"So what do you think?" asked Rhys after a tiny pause.

"Um...about a goodbye kiss?"

"Yes."

"Well, I...I suppose it wouldn't do any harm. I wasn't sure Kate was entirely convinced last night."

"That's what I thought."

Another silence, longer this time. Long enough for Thea to wonder if he could actually hear her pulse booming.

"We'd better make it look good then," said Rhys.

It was too much for Thea. As if of their own accord, her hands lifted to his arms, slid upwards to wind around his neck and pull him toward her. Or maybe she didn't need to pull him. Maybe Rhys was closing the distance anyway. But, however it happened, they were kissing at last, and the release from all that anticipation was so intense Thea gasped in spite of herself.

So much for cool, calm and in control.

Jessica Hart had a haphazard career before she began writing to finance a degree in history. Her experience ranged from waitress, theater production assistant and outback cook to newsdesk secretary, expedition assistant and English teacher, and she has worked in countries as different as France and Indonesia, Australia and Cameroon. She now lives in the north of England, where her hobbies are limited to eating and drinking and traveling when she can, preferably to places where she'll find good food or desert or tropical rain.

If you'd like to find out more about Jessica Hart, you can visit her Web site at www.jessicahart.co.uk

Books by Jessica Hart

HARLEQUIN ROMANCE®

3757—FIANCÉ WANTED FAST!*
3761—THE BLIND-DATE PROPOSAL*
3765—THE WHIRLWIND ENGAGEMENT*
3797—HER BOSS'S BABY PLAN

*CITY BRIDES trilogy

Christmas Eve Marriage

Jessica Hart

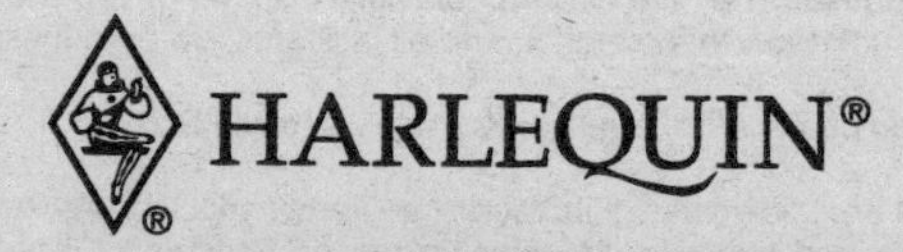

TORONTO • NEW YORK • LONDON
AMSTERDAM • PARIS • SYDNEY • HAMBURG
STOCKHOLM • ATHENS • TOKYO • MILAN • MADRID
PRAGUE • WARSAW • BUDAPEST • AUCKLAND

ISBN 0-373-03820-8

CHRISTMAS EVE MARRIAGE

First North American Publication 2004.

This edition published by arrangement with Harlequin Books S.A.

www.eHarlequin.com

Printed in U.S.A.

CHAPTER ONE

NOTHING.

Thea closed the fridge with a sigh and began investigating the kitchen cupboards, but they were equally empty of anything remotely resembling breakfast.

What a great start to the holiday! A nightmare journey, an unfriendly neighbour, less than four hours' sleep, and now nothing to eat.

'Have a fortnight in Crete, she said,' Thea muttered her sister's words as she bent to peer. 'You need a break. It'll be beautiful. Nothing to do but read, relax...starve to death...'

'What are you doing?'

Clara's voice made Thea straighten and push her tangled hair away from her face. Her niece was at the bottom of the stairs, looking sleepy and tousled and very sweet in a baggy pink T-shirt. There was no doubt that it was a look that was easier to pull off after four hours' sleep at nine, when you had peachy skin and a nice, firm little body, than at thirty-four, when peachy skin and a firm body had never figured largely among your assets in the first place.

'Trying to find some breakfast,' she said, yawning.

'Oh, good. I'm hungry.'

'Me too,' said Thea glumly.

Nothing new there, then. Easy to tell that she and Clara were related. You'd think they'd be too tired to be hungry. It had been nearly half past five before they got to bed that morning, and it was only just after nine now. Any normal stomach would be daunted by a nightmare trip, arriving in a strange country and utter exhaustion, but Martindale stomachs were tougher than that! A massive asteroid could be hurtling towards earth and her stomach would still be going, Mmm, nine o'clock, no wonder I'm a bit peckish... Bacon and eggs would be nice, or perhaps a little croissant before the end of the world... Oh, and make that a double cappuccino while you're at it.

She hadn't even lost weight over Harry. It wasn't fair. All her friends lost their appetites the moment they hit an emotional crisis, but the misery diet never worked for Thea. She just went in for comfort eating on a massive scale.

Not that there was much chance of eating now, worse luck.

'I can't find anything to eat,' she told Clara. 'I think we may have to go shopping before breakfast.'

Clara's face fell. 'But there aren't any shops here. We'll have to drive all the way back to that town we passed last night, and it'll take ages. It's *miles* away.'

'I know.' Thea grimaced at the memory of their hair-raising journey through the hills in the small hours. 'I'm not sure I can face those hairpin bends again, let alone on an empty stomach,' she said with a sigh.

'What shall we do?'

'Well, first I think we should ring your mother and ask her why she booked a villa in the middle of nowhere, instead of a nice beach apartment near shops and restaurants!'

Clara grinned. 'She did say it was isolated.'

'It's that all right.'

Thea eyed the view through the kitchen window without enthusiasm. Rocky hillsides, olive groves and the spectacular peaks of the White Mountains in the distance were all very well, but right then she would have sacrificed picturesque for the odd blot on the landscape, an ugly supermarket, say, or a nice plastic restaurant—preferably one that delivered coffee by the gallon and an assortment of calorie-laden breakfasts.

She nibbled her thumb as she tried to think, but her brain really needed caffeine before it would function properly.

'We're just going to have to ask the people in the other villas if they can let us have some bread or something until we can get to the shops,' she decided eventually.

'We don't have to ask that grumpy man we met last night, do we?'

Clara looked a little apprehensive, as well she might, thought Thea, remembering their disastrous arrival.

'I think there are three villas, aren't there? We'll try the other one first,' she said, trying to sound positive. 'Maybe they'll be friendlier.'

They couldn't be less friendly, anyway, she thought glumly. So much for her relaxing holiday. She hadn't planned to kick it off begging for a bit of bread and water. Why did these things happen to her?

Oh, well. Better get on with it.

They got dressed, which in Thea's case meant shorts and a T-shirt, while Clara simply pulled a T-shirt over her swimming costume, and then headed off in search of breakfast.

In spite of their hunger, they hesitated on the terrace and took in their surroundings. It was the first time they had seen the villas. Three stone-built houses were set around a communal pool that glinted bright and blue in the dazzling Greek sunlight.

'Cool,' breathed Clara. 'Can I swim after breakfast?'

It was very quiet. The air was already warm and filled with the drifting scent of herbs, and Thea sniffed appreciatively. 'Lovely…thyme and oregano…let's get some lamb to cook tonight.'

'Let's get breakfast first,' said the more practical Clara.

Their villa sat between the two others, looking directly

out over the pool to the mountains beyond. On the right was the villa they had stumbled into by mistake the night before.

'Let's try this way first,' said Thea, pointing left.

All was very quiet as they climbed the steps leading up to the terrace. 'Hello?' Thea called, but there was no reply. 'Hello?'

'I don't think there's anyone here,' Clara whispered, affected by the silence.

'It doesn't look like it.'

Reluctantly, as one, they turned to look at the villa opposite. They had a much better view across the pool than from their own terrace, and they could clearly see the man sitting at a table under a vine-laden pergola. A little girl was slumped in a chair beside him, scuffing her shoes sulkily.

'There he is.' This time it was Thea whispering.

'He still looks cross,' said Clara.

It was too far to read his expression, in fact, but Thea knew what her niece meant. There was something off-putting about the body language on the opposite terrace.

She bit her lip doubtfully. She had already experienced the rough side of his tongue, and she didn't fancy it again. OK, the mistake was theirs, but there had been no need for him to be quite that fierce, had there?

If she had any self-respect, she would go and find the car keys and brave the hairpin bends before she would ask him for so much as a glass of water.

It was a battle between pride and her stomach, and her stomach won. No surprises there then.

'He's probably got a nice wife inside,' she suggested to Clara. 'She might feel guilty about the way he shouted at us. We weren't making *that* much noise.'

'It was five in the morning,' said Clara gloomily. 'And you did crash into his car.'

'It was just a little bump.'

Clara's mouth turned down at the corners. 'Maybe we should go to that town after all,' she said, but Thea had stiffened.

'Look.' She nudged her niece as she spotted a cup and a cafetière on the table. 'He's got coffee!'

She felt quite giddy at the thought. She would do anything for a cup of coffee right then. 'Let's just go and see,' she encouraged Clara. 'He's not going to be rude in front of his little girl, is he?'

Clara was clearly unconvinced, but she could see that her aunt was determined. 'OK, but you do the talking,' she warned.

Buoyed up at the prospect of coffee, Thea bore her niece around the pool and back past their own villa. It was only at the bottom of the steps that her nerve began to fail. Close to, the man's face was very grim as he looked out at the view. He was evidently lost in his thoughts, and it didn't look as if they were particularly happy ones.

He hadn't seen them yet, and Thea faltered. 'Maybe this isn't such a good idea after all,' she muttered.

'Go on,' whispered Clara, giving her a push. 'We're here now, and I'm starving!'

Thea opened her mouth to argue, but just then the little girl spotted them and sat up curiously. She tugged at her father's sleeve, and he turned his head and saw them lurking at the bottom of the steps. The intimidating brows rose in surprise and Thea gulped. It was too late to turn and run now.

Squaring her shoulders, she trod up the steps with an assumption of confidence, Clara following reluctantly in her wake.

'Morning!' She produced a bright smile, the kind of smile she might give someone she had never met before. Someone who had never shouted at her furiously.

He looked a little taken aback by her smile as he got to his feet. 'Good morning.'

His voice was cool but civil. That was something, thought Thea, looking on the bright side. At least he hadn't leapt to his feet and roared at them the way he had only a matter of hours ago. It wasn't the warmest welcome she had ever received, but Thea had to admit that she probably didn't deserve one of those.

'Hello.' She smiled a little nervously at the little girl and received a blank stare in return. Oh. That grimness must run in the family.

She turned back to the man. 'We…er…thought we should come over and apologise for last night…well, this morning.'

Distracted by the smell of coffee, her gaze wandered in spite of herself over to the cafetière, and she had to force herself to look back at him. 'I'm very sorry for waking you up and…er…and for crashing into your car.'

To her surprise, the sternness in his face lightened somewhat. 'I think I'm the one who should apologise,' he said. 'I'm afraid I was very rude to you. I'd had a difficult day,' he went on, his own gaze straying involuntarily towards his daughter, 'and an even worse evening, so I was in a filthy temper long before you arrived. It wasn't fair to take it out on you.'

An apology from him was the last thing Thea had expected, and she was completely thrown. 'I don't blame you for being annoyed,' she said, stammering slightly. 'It was very late and we were making a lot of noise, I know.

'It was just that we'd had such a nightmare journey,' she tried to explain. 'The plane was delayed, of course, and then there was some problem with the baggage handling at the airport, which meant that we had to wait ages for our cases. By the time we'd found the car hire place, I was so tired I was like some kind of zombie—and that was before we had to find our way here in the dark.'

'It's not an easy drive at the best of times,' he said, which was nice of him, Thea thought. Especially when she doubted very much that he would have found it difficult at any time of day. He had an air of calm competence about him that could be intimidating or incredibly reassuring, depending on how much you really needed someone competent with you.

'I'd no idea it would be so far, or that the roads would be that scary,' she told him. 'It's not as if I'm a good driver to begin with—I'm more used to taking cabs—and I really thought we'd never get here. We'd been creeping along for miles in the dark, terrified we were going to go over the edge…don't you think somebody would have thought of putting up safety barriers at some point?…and it was such a relief to get here at last that I probably stopped concentrating.

'We came round that corner there,' she went on, pointing. 'And the next thing I knew there was this big bang. I didn't see your car until it was too late. I wasn't going that fast,' she added guiltily and risked a glance at him. Fortunately he was looking more amused than anything. Phew. A big change from last night!

'It was just a little bump really, but I suppose it was the last straw. We were both so tired by then that we started to laugh. It was that or cry.'

'So that's what all the giggling was about,' he said dryly. 'I wondered what was so funny.'

'I think it was hysteria rather than amusement, but once we'd started laughing we couldn't stop. You know what it's like when you start snorting, and then you set each other off…' Thea trailed off as she realised that he was just looking at her.

No, of course he didn't. Obviously not.

'Well...anyway...we didn't realise how much noise we were making, obviously,' she hurried on. 'And then when we found ourselves in the wrong villa, it just seemed even funnier.'

Or had, until he had come roaring down the stairs and demanded to know what the hell they thought they were doing. He had been furious. As well he might be, Thea thought contritely. If she'd been woken up in the early hours of the morning by the sound of someone crashing into her car, and if they had then started fooling around, laughing loudly and breaking into her house, she probably wouldn't have been that amused either.

'I'm really sorry,' she said, wondering why it suddenly seemed so important to convince him that she wasn't as silly as she had been last night. Or not often, anyway.

'Forget it,' he said. 'It wasn't your fault that I'd completely mislaid my sense of humour last night. I think we should pretend that we've never clapped eyes on each other before and start again, don't you?'

'That's very nice of you.' Thea smiled gratefully at him. 'I'm Thea Martindale, and this is my niece, Clara.'

'Rhys Kingsford.'

Nice hands, Thea thought involuntarily as they shook hands. Warm, firm, capable. No clamminess or knobbly knuckles or suggestive little squeezes. Yes, full marks on the hand front.

And the rest of him was bearing up well to closer scrutiny as well. A bit severe-looking maybe, with those dark brows and stern features, but he was certainly more attractive than she had realised last night. Not handsome like Harry, of course—no one was as good-looking as Harry—but still... yes, definitely attractive.

Certainly attractive enough for Thea to wish that she had

taken the time to brush her hair properly and put on something more flattering before she came out.

Rhys was gesturing towards the little girl who was still sitting at the table, refusing to show the slightest interest in what was going on. 'My daughter, Sophie.'

'Hi, Sophie,' said Thea, and Clara smiled in a friendly fashion.

His mouth thinned somewhat as she merely hunched a shoulder. 'Say hello, Sophie,' he said, a note of warning in his voice.

''lo,' she muttered.

A muscle beat in his jaw, but he turned back to Thea and smiled with an obvious attempt to master his frustration. 'Well...how about some coffee? There's plenty in the pot and it's still hot.'

Thea had been afraid he would never ask. The relationship between Rhys and his daughter was obviously strained but she was slavering too much over the smell of coffee to make a polite excuse and leave them to sort out their differences.

'That would be lovely,' she said firmly before the invitation could be withdrawn. 'Actually, we came over to ask if you could possibly spare us some bread or something for breakfast,' she went on in response to a nudge from Clara. 'We haven't got anything in the villa, and it's a long drive to the shops.'

'Of course,' said Rhys. 'Sophie, why don't you go and see what you can find for breakfast—and bring a cup for Thea.'

Sophie's brows drew together mutinously, and for a moment she looked uncannily like her father had earlier that morning. 'I don't know where the cups are.'

'Try looking in the cupboard,' he told her, keeping his temper with an effort. 'There's some bread and jam on the table. You could bring that out, and whatever Clara would like to drink.'

'I'll help you,' offered Clara quickly as Sophie opened her mouth to protest.

Sophie looked deeply suspicious, but after a glance at her implacable father she deigned to drag herself off her chair and scuffed her way inside, accompanied by an unfazed Clara.

There was a slightly awkward pause. 'Sorry about that,' said Rhys, running an exasperated hand through his hair and gesturing for Thea to sit down. 'She's going through a difficult phase at the moment.'

'How old is she?' Thea hoped she would hurry back with that cup. That coffee smell was driving her wild.

'Nearly eight.'

'Clara's nine. They should get on like a house on fire.'

He sighed. 'I'm not sure Sophie gets on with anybody at the moment.'

'Well, Clara gets on with everybody,' said Thea cheerfully. 'I bet you anything that they're friends in no time.'

Rhys looked as if he wanted to believe her, but couldn't quite let himself. 'Clara seems a very nice little girl,' he said.

'She is,' said Thea with an affectionate smile. 'It's a bit disheartening sometimes to find that your nine-year-old niece is more sensible than you are, but apart from that she's a star! She's great company too. It's easy to forget that she's only nine sometimes.'

'Is it just the two of you on holiday?'

'Yes. Clara was supposed to be coming with my sister but Nell slipped off some steps at the beach three weeks ago and managed to break a foot and a wrist, which means she's been effectively immobilised ever since. There was no question of her being able to drive or walk, so she'd have been completely stuck up here, even if she'd been able to get here in the first place.'

'Unfortunate,' said Rhys. 'Was she insured?'

Thea nodded. 'Oh, yes, Nell's always very sensible about things like that. I'm sure she would have been able to claim the cost of cancelling the holiday, but Clara would have been so disappointed. She's been looking forward to this for ages. Her father never takes her on holiday.'

She scowled, thinking about her sister's ex-husband. 'He's got a new family now, and his new wife doesn't like Clara very much. I think she's probably jealous of her.'

'Clara's parents are divorced?' Rhys looked surprised. 'She seems so…happy.'

'She's fine,' said Thea. 'She was very small when Simon left, so she's always taken the fact that her parents live separately for granted. She sees Simon regularly, and Nell's been very careful not to expose her to any bitterness.'

'Maybe she and Clara will have something in common after all.'

Ah. Thea had been wondering about Sophie's mother. 'You're divorced as well?'

He nodded, his face set. 'Sophie hasn't adjusted as well as Clara, though. She wasn't even two when Lynda left, so she's not used to us living together either.

'I was working in North Africa at the time,' he went on. 'My work took me to the desert a lot and Lynda said it wasn't a suitable place to bring up a child. I suppose it was difficult for her, but…'

His mouth twisted slightly at the memory and he made a visible effort to shrug it aside. 'Anyway, she came home and we divorced. Nobody else was involved, and it was as free of bitterness as a divorce can be. We're still on good terms.'

'That must make it easier for Sophie, doesn't it?'

'The trouble is that I've seen so little of her.' Rhys drank his coffee morosely. 'My job kept me in Morocco for another five years. Whenever I had leave and could get back to the UK, I saw Sophie, of course, but it wasn't that often, and I guess I am pretty much a stranger to her.'

'That must be hard,' said Thea carefully.

His mouth turned down as he nodded. 'The last time I came home, I realised that I didn't know my daughter at all, and I didn't want it to be like that. I want to be a proper father to her, not just someone who turns up with presents every now and then. So I got myself a job in London, where I could live nearby, and I'm trying to see her more regularly now, but…'

'But what?' she prompted. 'It sounds to me as if you did exactly the right thing.'

'I'm just afraid I may have left it too late,' said Rhys reluctantly. 'I know I only came back a few weeks ago, but it's as if Sophie is determined not to be won over.'

'It might take a little time,' said Thea, hearing the hurt in his voice. 'It's probably confusing for her too, to suddenly have a full-time father.'

'I suppose so.' He sighed and raked a hand through his hair in a weary gesture. 'I was hoping that coming away on holiday together would be a good chance for us to get to know each other properly and get used to each other, but it hasn't been a great success so far. I imagined us going for long walks together and talking, but Sophie doesn't like walking and half the time she won't talk to me either. She says she's bored.'

'Aren't there any other children here?'

'Yes, there are two boys staying in the other villa.' Rhys nodded across the pool. 'Unfortunately, they're very well behaved. Sophie says they're boring, too.'

'I'm sure Clara will sort them all out,' said Thea comfortably as Sophie came back out on to the terrace, looking marginally less sullen.

She thrust a cup at Thea. 'Here.'

'Thanks.' Thea took it with a smile. Clara would have known that her aunt was desperate for coffee, she thought gratefully, but Rhys was frowning at his daughter's gracelessness.

'What about a saucer?' he asked, but Sophie was already on her way back to the kitchen.

'Honestly, this is fine,' said Thea quickly before he followed her. It was all she could do to contain herself as Rhys poured coffee into her cup.

'That smells wonderful.' She sighed, breathing in deeply. 'Mmm....' She took a sip and closed her eyes blissfully. 'God, that tastes good!'

Lowering the cup, she smiled at Rhys, a wide, warm smile that lit up her face and left him looking oddly startled for a moment. 'I've been fantasising about this all morning!'

He raised a brow. 'Nice to meet a woman whose fantasies are so easily satisfied!' he said dryly.

His eyes were an unusual greenish-grey colour, their paleness striking in his brown face. Thea was surprised that she hadn't noticed them before, and, distracted, it took her a moment to register what he had said.

A faint flush stained her cheeks when she did, and she made herself look away. 'Some of them, anyway.'

There was a pause while Thea drank her coffee and gazed studiously at the view, wishing she could think of something to say.

The sudden silence was interrupted, much to her relief, by Sophie and Clara, bearing breakfast. Bread and jam were laid carefully on the table, along with some ripe peaches, a pot of Greek yoghurt and some honey.

'This looks wonderful, Sophie,' said Thea, although she

was fairly sure that her practical niece had taken a leading role in procuring the lavish spread. Sophie had that pale, thin look of a child with no interest in food. 'Thank you so much.'

Sophie hunched a shoulder in acknowledgment and resumed her slumped posture on the chair, but Thea noticed that, beneath her fringe, her eyes were alert as she watched them tucking into breakfast with relish.

Rhys watched them too, with quiet amusement. 'It's a pleasure to see girls with such healthy appetites,' he said as Thea poured honey over a bowlful of yoghurt, handing it to Clara before preparing one of her own.

'We're very hungry,' she said a little defensively. 'We haven't eaten since the meal on the plane, have we, Clara?'

Clara shook her head, her mouth full. 'This is so good,' she said when she could. 'Can we have yoghurt and honey for breakfast every day?'

'Sure,' said Thea. 'We'll get some when we replace everything we've eaten now.'

'Don't worry about it,' said Rhys, resigned. 'I bought most of it for Sophie, anyway. I thought it would be good to have a real Greek breakfast, but she won't touch it, will you?' he added to his daughter.

Sophie's lower lip stuck out. 'Mum doesn't eat dairy products, so why should I have to?'

'No dairy products?' Thea stared at her, appalled. 'No cheese? No milk? No butter?'

'Or red meat or potatoes or bread or salt…' Rhys said, sounding tired.

That was Thea's entire diet out of the window then. 'Chocolate? Biscuits?' She didn't even think it was worth mentioning alcohol.

His smile twisted. 'You're kidding, aren't you? Lynda's

permanently on some faddy diet or another. She's obsessive about every mouthful.'

No wonder Sophie had looked so surprised when she saw them guzzling breakfast. Imagine having that kind of self-control.

'She must have a lovely figure,' said Thea, wishing she hadn't had quite such a large bowl of yoghurt.

Sophie nodded. 'She does.'

'I think she's too thin,' said Rhys.

Thea tried to imagine anyone saying that about her. *The thing about Thea is she's just too thin.* No, it just didn't sound right. Totally unconvincing, in fact. A bit like saying, *The thing about George Clooney is he's just too ugly.*

On the other hand, it sounded as if Rhys might actually prefer his women to have a few more curves than a stick insect. That was good.

Whoops, where had *that* thought come from? Thea caught herself up guiltily. She wasn't the slightest bit interested in how he liked his women.

'I wish I had that kind of self-discipline,' she said with a sigh. 'I'm always trying to diet, but I'm lucky if I make it to lunch without devouring a packet of Hob Nobs to make up for just a grapefruit for breakfast.'

'You don't need to diet,' Clara leapt in loyally. 'Mum says you're silly to worry about your weight. She says you've got a sexy figure and men much prefer that to thin girls.'

'Clara!' Mortified, Thea tried to kick her under the table.

'Well, she does,' insisted Clara, and then made things a million times worse by turning to Rhys. 'It's true, isn't it?'

'Clara…'

Unperturbed by the directness of the question, Rhys had turned and was studying Thea. 'I think your mother's right,' he said, straight-faced, and Clara sat back, satisfied.

'See?' she said to Thea, who was blushing furiously.

'If you've finished your breakfast, maybe you'd like to go and have a swim?' she suggested through her teeth.

'Cool!' Clara leapt to her feet. 'Come on, Sophie.'

Sophie looked warily at her father. 'Can I go?'

'Of course,' he said, and she slid off her chair and ran after Clara.

Thea buried her burning face in her coffee cup, but when she risked a glance at him saw that the disconcerting eyes were green and light with amusement.

'Is she always that direct?'

'If I didn't love her so much, I could kill her sometimes!' Thea gave in and laughed. 'She can be disastrously honest, and if she likes you she'll stop at nothing to get you what you want—or what she thinks you need!'

She shook her head ruefully. 'Clara's like her mother that way. They're both so determined, it's often easiest just to give in and do as they say!'

A smile twitched at the corner of Rhys's mouth. 'What if they don't like you? Does it work the other way?'

'Unfortunately, yes.' Thea's own smile faded as she remembered how much Nell and Clara had disliked Harry. She had never been able to understand that. Harry was so good-looking and charming. How could anyone *not* like him?

'I'd keep on her good side if I were you,' she said to Rhys, and the intriguing dent at the corner of his mouth deepened in amusement.

'I'll remember that. Now, how about some fresh coffee?' He picked up the cafetière and waved it tantalisingly.

'Well...' She didn't want to seem too greedy.

'Go on, fulfil those fantasies! You know you want it,' he tempted her, and smiled at her, a swift and totally unexpected smile that illuminated his face and left Thea with the peculiar sensation of having missed a step as her breath stumbled.

She swallowed. 'That would be lovely.'

The coffee smelt just as good as before when he came back, but this time Thea was less easily distracted by it. She found herself studying him under her lashes instead as he sat back in his chair, hands curled around his cup, watching the girls in the pool.

He wasn't *that* attractive, not really. He was compactly-built and obviously fit, and he had that air of toughness and confidence she associated with men who spent most of their life outdoors. He had mentioned working in the desert, and Thea could imagine him in a wild setting like that, unfazed by the heat and the emptiness of the elements as he narrowed his eyes at the far horizon.

Of course, it might just be the tan that made her think that.

Her gaze dropped to his hands, and the memory of how his palm had felt touching hers was enough to send a tiny shiver down her spine. Yes, nice hands, nice eyes.

Nice mouth, too, now she came to think of it. Cool and firm looking, with just a hint of sensuousness about the bottom lip. It was a shame it seemed normally set in such a stern line, but the effect when he smiled was literally breathtaking.

Hmm.

Thea was uneasily aware that her hormones, long fixated on Harry, were definitely stirring and taking an interest. Odd. She frowned slightly. Rhys wasn't her type at all. He couldn't have been more different from Harry.

She shifted in her chair, trying to shake the feeling off. Maybe it was the sleepless night catching up on her, she thought hopefully, although she was definitely feeling better after that breakfast.

'Listen!' Rhys sat forward suddenly, startling Thea out of her thoughts.

'What?'

'Sophie's laughing.'

CHAPTER TWO

THERE was such an odd note in his voice that Thea looked to where the two little girls were running around the pool and dive-bombing with much shrieking and giggling.

'They'll be inseparable now,' she said. 'I'm afraid you won't see nearly so much of her.'

'I don't mind as long as she's happy.'

Something about his expression made Thea's heart twist. Underneath that tough exterior, he was clearly vulnerable about his daughter. He struck her as the kind of man who would dismiss emotions as 'touchy feely', but it was easy to see that he loved Sophie desperately and was bothered more than he cared to admit by his inability to bond with her.

And Sophie obviously wasn't making it easy for him. Remembering that sullen expression and the stubborn set to that little chin, Thea couldn't help feeling that he had a long way to go. She felt sorry for him.

Which was much better than feeling disturbed by him.

Draining her coffee, she pushed back her chair. 'Thank you so much for breakfast,' she said gratefully. 'I feel as if I can face that awful drive now that I've got some caffeine inside me. I was dreading getting back in the car again.'

'If it's any help, I'm going down myself in a bit,' he said casually, getting to his feet at the same time. 'We need to stock up as well, so I could give you a lift if you really don't like the idea of driving.'

She really *didn't*, but Thea hesitated. 'That would be wonderful,' she said, trying not to sound too eager. 'I feel as if I'd be exploiting you, though. So far you've provided breakfast and coffee, and all I've done is wake you up in the middle of the night and crash into your car. It's rather a one-sided relationship, isn't it?' she joked a little uneasily.

For answer, Rhys cocked his ear in the direction of the pool where the girls could be heard giggling together. 'That's the first time Sophie has laughed in a week,' he said simply. 'She actually sounds as if she's enjoying herself. A pot of yoghurt, a cup of coffee and a lift into town when I was going anyway doesn't seem much compared to that.'

'Well, if you're sure...' Thea let herself be persuaded. Pride had never been her strong point anyway, and there was no point in both of them driving down that road again, was there?

'That's settled then,' said Rhys briskly. 'If I can persuade the girls out of the pool, will you be ready to leave in half an hour?'

'Half an hour's fine,' she said, calculating that would give her plenty of time to change. She wasn't sitting next to Rhys in these shorts, that was for sure.

Oh, to have lovely long, slender thighs that you could flaunt without worrying about how they would look splayed out over the passenger seat. The only alternative was to sit with her feet braced to keep the weight off her thighs, and that drive was stressful enough as it was. The last thing she needed was the added anxiety of keeping cellulite under control.

Not that there was any reason to suppose that Rhys would even notice what her thighs were doing.

Or for her to care whether he did or not.

It was just habit, Thea told herself, frantically dragging clothes out of her case. She had been in no state to unpack when they arrived in the early hours, and now everything was disastrously crumpled. She was used to constantly fretting about her appearance with Harry, who was super-critical and forever remembering how beautifully groomed Isabelle was.

The thought of Harry and Isabelle made her wince, but it wasn't that awful lacerating pain it had once been. The realisation made Thea pause. Perhaps Nell had been right when she said a change of scenery was what Thea needed.

'There's no point in moping around while you wait for Harry to make up his mind,' her sister had said. 'Go somewhere different. Think about something different.'

Like the smile in Rhys's eyes and the feel of his hand touching hers.

Thea went back to pulling clothes out of her case, but more slowly. Yes, maybe Nell had a point. Coming out to Crete in Nell's place had forced her out of her rut. It had been so long since she had been anywhere new, met anyone new, thought about anything other than Harry that her reactions were all over the place.

That would explain her peculiar physical reaction to Rhys, wouldn't it? She wasn't *attracted* to him. No, she was simply adjusting to the unfamiliar, and obviously lack of sleep—not to mention acute caffeine deprivation—hadn't helped her behave normally.

Still, that was no reason not to look her best. She would feel more herself when she was properly dressed. But in what?

'Dress or skirt and top?' Thea held the alternative outfits up for Clara's inspection when her niece appeared, still dripping from the pool.

Clara considered. 'The dress is pretty, but it's all creased.'

'Linen's supposed to look a bit creased,' said Thea, relieved to have had the decision made for her. Clara had her mother's taste and even as a very little girl her opinion had been worth having.

Tossing aside the skirt and top, she rummaged around in her case for a pair of strappy sandals. 'It's part of its charm.'

'Are we going out?'

'Didn't Rhys tell you? He's giving us a lift to the supermarket in that town we passed.'

Clara eyed her aunt suspiciously. 'Why are you getting dressed up to go shopping?'

'I'm only putting on a dress!' Thea protested.

'And you've got lipstick on.'

Trust Clara to notice that. 'I often wear lipstick. It doesn't mean anything.'

'Rhys is nice, isn't he?'

It was Thea's turn to look suspicious at the airy change of subject. 'He seems nice, yes.'

'Do you think he's good-looking?'

'He's OK,' said Thea. Nothing like Harry, of course, but yes, definitely OK.

She didn't want Clara matchmaking, though. Her niece didn't like Harry and was tireless in suggesting alternative boyfriends—encouraged by her mother, Thea thought darkly. If Clara got it into her head that Rhys would do for her aunt, she would be shameless in promoting their relationship, and Thea could foresee huge potential for embarrassment.

'Sophie says he's really cross the whole time,' Clara was continuing artlessly, 'but he didn't seem cross to me. He's got lovely smiley eyes.'

Thea didn't feel like admitting that she had noticed his eyes herself. 'Really?' she said discouragingly instead.

'Maybe he could be your boyfriend?' Clara suggested, evidently deciding to go for the direct approach after all. 'Sophie says he hasn't got a girlfriend.'

Thea filed that little piece of information away to consider when her niece's gimlet eyes weren't fixed upon her.

'I'm not looking for a boyfriend,' she said firmly. 'You know I'm still in love with Harry. You don't get over somebody just like that.'

Clara set her chin stubbornly. 'Rhys would be much better for you than Harry,' she said, sounding so like her mother that Thea was quite taken aback.

'Well, I'm sorry to disappoint you, but I'm afraid he's not really my type,' she said, wishing that Clara would go so that she could check her make-up.

Just because Rhys wasn't her type didn't mean she should let standards slip.

'I think you should give him a try. I'm sure he'd be nicer to you than Harry.'

'Clara, we're going shopping not embarking on a new relationship, all right? And if you *dare* say anything like that to Rhys or Sophie, I'll...I'll be very cross,' she finished in a threatening voice that had absolutely no effect on her niece, who grinned and skipped out of the room to change out of her wet swimming costume.

Without making any promises at all, Thea noticed.

Rhys had hired a sturdy 4x4 which dwarfed the tinny little model Thea had driven up the road in the small hours. She eyed its gleaming exterior nervously. It looked like an expensive car to repair.

'Did I do any damage last night?'

'Barely a scratch, in spite of all that noise,' said Rhys, giving the bonnet an affectionate slap, much as he might pat a horse. 'She's solid as anything. It might be worth checking your own bumpers, though.'

'I'll do that when we get back,' said Thea vaguely, with no intention of doing anything of the kind. She would worry about any damage when she returned the car. For now, she would be quite happy if she didn't have to go anywhere near it for the next two weeks.

Thea enjoyed the drive much more than she had expected to. It was wonderful not having to worry about the lack of safety barriers or the precipitous drops, or being responsible for getting the car round each of the tortuous bends. She could sit back, relax and enjoy the view.

Or she would have been able to if only she could stop her eyes drifting over to Rhys. He was an incredibly calm and reassuring driver. Unlike her, he didn't get his gears muddled up. He didn't shout at the car or swear or panic about which side of the road he was supposed to be driving on. He just sat there, hands sure and steady on the steering wheel, and Thea felt utterly safe in a way she never had with Harry, who drove a flash model and couldn't bear to have another car on the road in front of him.

Rhys was the kind of person you wanted to be sitting next to on a plane when both pilots went down with some mysterious disease and all the passengers were left to panic. Thea had seen a late-night movie like that once. Everyone flapped around and in the end the heroine had to get the plane down, but if Rhys had been there things would have been different. He would have taken over the controls and calmly landed the plane.

Of course, it wouldn't have made for such an exciting movie.

On the other hand, if the director added in fizzing sexual tension between Rhys and the heroine, who probably bore an uncanny resemblance to Thea herself, it might work. The two of them could end up shut in a room together—quarantine, Thea decided, blithely disposing of all the other passengers—and someone would have made a mistake so there was just a double bed and neither of them would have any pyjamas with them, naturally, and Rhys would say, Well, no point in wasting it, is there? At which point *she*…

Good grief, what was she *thinking* about? Thea jerked

herself back from the brink of fantasy just in time. For a moment there she had felt quite…hot.

This getting-out-of-a-rut business was doing very odd things to those hormones of hers. From having their interest piqued earlier over breakfast, they were now standing up, putting on their lipstick and patting their hair into place, ready for action.

Down, girls, Thea told them sternly. Concentrate on the view instead.

Fortunately, Clara was chatting away with her usual disarming friendliness in the back seat. Thea herself felt too shaky to carry on a conversation. It was all she could do to stare unseeingly out of the window and will her hormones to relapse into lethargy once more.

'Don't worry, we'll be there soon.' Rhys's voice made her start.

'What?'

He smiled. 'You're looking a bit nervous. The worst of the road is over now.'

'Oh. Right. Yes.' Thea cleared her throat. 'I suppose I was a bit nervous.'

That was true enough, but it wasn't about the lack of safety barriers.

Once at the supermarket, they split up. Sophie trailed listlessly behind her father, responding to his suggestions about what she would like to eat with her usual hunched shoulder.

'Whatever,' was all she would say, while Clara and Thea puzzled over the Greek alphabet.

'We'll just have to go by the pictures,' said Thea, tossing what she hoped was a tin of tuna into the trolley. It was either that or pilchards.

'I think Rhys really likes you,' whispered Clara in a stage whisper. 'I saw the way he was smiling at you in the car.'

'Shh!' Thea glared at her, pointing frantically to indicate that Rhys and Sophie might be in the next aisle.

'We should invite them to dinner,' Clara pursued in the same stage whisper, ignoring her.

Thea closed her eyes briefly. 'Clara, I really don't think—'

'To thank them for breakfast and giving us a lift,' Clara added innocently. 'I'm sure Mum would say we should.'

She would, too. 'We're on holiday. We don't want to spend a lot of time cooking,' said Thea, conscious that she was fighting a losing battle.

'I'll help you. We just need to make something simple. Sophie says her dad's always going on about how he likes home cooking, but he can only do about three things himself. He'd probably really like it if you cooked something for him.'

In the end, Thea gave in to shut Clara up. She knew quite well that her niece had visions of whisking Sophie away so that she and Rhys would be left sharing a romantic dinner for two on the terrace in the dark, with just the stars for company.

Put like that, it didn't sound too bad, did it? Thea's hormones rustled with something dangerously like excitement at the thought. They were completely out of order today.

Besides, Clara was right. A meal in return for all Rhys's help was the least she could offer. She would make the invitation very casual. If he didn't want to come, she would have done her duty and she could tell Clara that Rhys wasn't really interested.

But when she mentioned it, as casually as she could, Rhys didn't even put up a token show of reluctance. 'That sounds great,' he said. 'We'd like that, wouldn't we, Sophie?'

'Better than eating with stupid Damian and Hugo,' she muttered.

Thea raised her brows at Rhys, who was looking uncomfortable at his daughter's lack of manners. 'Damian and Hugo?'

'The two boys in the other villa,' he explained. 'The Paines are here for three weeks as well. They've been very hospitable all week, a little too hospitable as far as Sophie's concerned. They're always asking us over for meals.'

'You don't like them either,' said Sophie sullenly.

'That's not true,' he protested, although not very convincingly, Thea thought.

They were sitting at a taverna in the village square, under the shade of an enormous plane tree. The shopping had been safely stashed in the car, and Thea was starving again. When Rhys had suggested lunch she had agreed with alacrity and had ordered *souvlaki* and chips with an enormous Greek salad, reasoning that it was too late to start pretending that a lettuce leaf was all she usually had for lunch, with perhaps a low fat yoghurt if she was indulging herself.

'Well, Clara and I are very honoured that you'd rather eat with us than Hugo and Damian, Sophie,' she said lightly, and Sophie hung her head.

'Yes, I would. Thanks,' she mumbled from behind her hair.

'It'll be great,' said Clara. 'Can Sophie and I go shopping?'

'Shopping?' Thea stared at her niece. 'Where?'

'They had some postcards at the supermarket.'

Thea strongly suspected that Clara was concocting an excuse to leave her alone with Rhys, but she could hardly accuse her of that now. She contented herself with a meaningful look.

'All right, but don't be too long, and stay together.'

'OK. Come on, Sophie.'

She bore Sophie off on a wave of enthusiasm that poor

Sophie was powerless to resist, and Thea and Rhys were left alone.

There was a slightly awkward silence. For some reason Thea's nerve endings were on alert, only amber so far, perhaps, but with those treacherous hormones egging them on Thea couldn't discount the alarming possibility that they would suddenly switch to red alert and start shrieking like an intruder alarm at a high security facility.

Desperately, she gazed around the village square but, stare as hard as she might at the whitewashed walls and the dusty geraniums straggling out of painted oil barrels and the gnarled old men sitting morosely in the shade, her attention was fixated on Rhys.

He was sitting next to her at the small square table, resting his forearms tantalisingly close to hers on the checked plastic tablecloth. Thea was acutely aware of the soft, dark hairs by his broad wrist, of the unpretentious watch, and the square, capable hands, and her fingers tingled with speculation about how it would feel to lay her own over them.

The very idea made the breath dry in her throat. Something was very wrong, she thought, confused. Her body appeared to have forgotten that she was pining for Harry. It was *Harry* whose warm skin she wanted to touch.

Only yesterday, Harry had dominated her thoughts, and now when she made the effort to conjure up his handsome face all she could see was Rhys, turning his head to smile at her, the sunlight in his eyes.

Thea felt as if the earth beneath her feet had suddenly started to crumble. She was just tired, she told herself desperately. How could she be thinking clearly after less than four hours' sleep? She would be fine after a siesta.

The waiter brought a little jug of retsina, and Thea tried not to stare at Rhys's hand as he poured, but her own was unsteady as she picked up her drink and their eyes met as they chinked glasses. She must get a grip.

Looking quickly away, she reached out for a fat green olive. 'Is it true what Sophie said?'

'What about?'

'That you don't like our neighbours? What are they called again…the Paines?'

'Oh, that.' Rhys looked a little uncomfortable. He swirled the liquid in his glass as he picked his words with care. 'They're very…kind,' he said at last.

'But?'

He grimaced. 'They're just a bit much, I suppose. Especially Kate. She's one of those women who believe everybody ought to be part of a couple, and seems to take the fact that I haven't married again as a personal affront. I'm not sure where she thinks I would have found a suitable wife in the Sahara!' he added dryly.

'Oh, God,' groaned Thea. 'Don't tell me I've come all the way to Crete to end up next to the kind of people who think being single is just a deliberately selfish attempt to throw out the seating plans for their dinner parties?'

The creases around Rhys's eyes deepened in amusement. 'Oh, you've met them, then?'

Glumly, Thea helped herself to another olive. 'They're part of an extended sub-species, *copulus smugus*, otherwise known as smug married couples.' She sighed. 'Oh, well, I suppose forewarned is forearmed,' she went on as she discarded the stone. 'I'll be ready for pitying looks and questions about why I haven't married and advice about not leaving it too long to have babies, because time's ticking away, isn't it?'

'I can't believe you'd get those kind of comments very often,' said Rhys, and she stared at him.

'Why not?'

He looked a bit taken aback by her vehemence. 'Well...I don't know. I'd just assumed that someone like you would always be with somebody.'

Someone like you. What did *that* mean?

'No, I seem to be a serial singleton.' Thea picked up her retsina and drank morosely.

The truth was that even when she had been with Harry she had never really felt part of a couple. She had kept waiting for someone to point a finger and say, Who do you think you're kidding? You're just playing at having a man.

Rhys was studying her vivid face over the rim of his own glass, noting the cloud of soft brown hair, the smoke-grey eyes, the generous curve of her mouth and the lush body. 'You surprise me,' he said.

Thea hadn't been expecting that. Startled, her eyes veered towards his and then skidded away. That smiling green gaze of his was unnerving enough at the best of times.

He was only being polite, anyway. What else could he say? Lose a couple of stone and do something about your hair, and you might be in with a chance?

She sipped her retsina, willing the faint colour across her cheekbones to fade. 'At least you're divorced,' she said. 'I've always assumed that would be better. And you've got a child, too. You don't need to prove you're normal!'

'Don't you believe it!' said Rhys with a twisted smile. 'Kate is on a mission now to fix me up with another wife. Every time we go over for a meal she tells me about another "awfully nice" friend of hers she thinks I would like.'

'Can't you just not go?'

'It's difficult. The Paines are friends of Lynda's—that's how we ended up here. I haven't been back in London that long, and the summer holidays seemed like a good opportunity to take Sophie away and spend a proper chunk of time together. It suited Lynda, too. She had some conference or something to go to, so we agreed that I would have Sophie for three weeks.'

'It's a very isolated place to spend three weeks,' commented Thea. 'I think I'd have taken her to somewhere more lively.'

Rhys nodded ruefully. 'That's what I should have done, but I didn't even think about going to a resort. I thought a beach would get really boring. You can't just lie in the sun for three weeks.'

Couldn't you? Thea looked at him. He was obviously one of those hearty ten-mile walk before breakfast types who always liked to be doing things. The art of lying on a sunbed and flicking through magazines with nothing more strenuous to do than contemplate what to eat and drink next would be quite lost on him. Shame, really.

'If I'd been a more hands-on father I'd have known what Sophie would like.' Rhys was frowning down at his glass. 'As it was, Lynda told me that the villa here was available because the friends who were originally coming out with the Paines had dropped out.

'It seemed like a good idea at the time,' he went on, lifting his eyes to Thea once more, obviously trying to justify the decision to himself. 'I thought that if the Paines were friends of Lynda's, Sophie would know the children and be able to play with them, but as it turned out they've got absolutely nothing in common.

'Meanwhile, Kate and Nick are desperate to look after us. Lynda obviously confides in Kate—she seems to know an unnerving amount about my marriage and divorce—and because they're friends, short of being outright rude, I can't get out of it.'

'It sounds a bit of a nightmare,' said Thea sympathetically.

'It is,' said Rhys, reaching for the jug of retsina and topping up her glass. 'Kate's impervious to hints that I'm quite capable of looking after myself. She went on and on about all these single friends of hers she wants to introduce me to when we get home, and I could foresee endless dinner parties if I didn't put a stop to it. Eventually I just told her I had met someone special already and that I was committed to her.'

Thea was conscious of a sinking feeling in the pit of her stomach that she didn't want to analyse. 'Oh,' she said. 'Have you?'

He gave a short, mirthless laugh. 'When would I have been able to meet anyone, let alone anyone special? I've been working in the middle of the desert for most of the past five years, and in the few weeks I've been back every minute of my time has been taken up with settling into a new job, buying and moving into a house and trying to coax two words out of my daughter.'

'You lied,' said Thea admiringly, trying to ignore the sudden lightening of her spirits at the news that Rhys did not, in fact, have a girlfriend.

'I had to,' he said, assuming a mock martyred expression, and she laughed as she picked up her drink once more.

'Well, thanks for the tip. I might invent an adoring fiancé back home myself before Kate gets me in her clutches!'

'Unless you'd like to be my girlfriend?' said Rhys.

Thea paused with the glass halfway to her lips. 'Sorry?'

'Well, if we're both going to pretend, we might as well back each other up,' he pointed out. 'If my supposed girlfriend was here in person, that would really shut Kate up.'

'But she'd know that I wasn't your girlfriend,' objected Thea, not entirely sure whether he was joking or not.

'How? I've never told her a name or anything about my girlfriend other than the fact that she exists, and Kate doesn't know who was booked into the villa. She told me herself that she was wondering who would turn up and hoping that it would be a ''nice family''. They didn't see you arrive last night, and they were off on some day trip before you got up, so she still doesn't know how disappointed she's going to be.'

His face seemed straight, but that was definitely an ironic gleam in those disconcertingly light eyes, and Thea was pretty sure she had seen the corner of his mouth twitch. So he *was* joking.

Phew.

She thought.

Sipping her retsina, she decided that she might as well enter into the spirit of the thing. It was just a joke, after all.

'Wouldn't you have told her I was coming?'

'Maybe you decided to surprise me?'

Thea laughed. 'What, by barging into the middle of the holiday you'd planned to spend alone with your daughter? I think that's a bit tactless, don't you? Frankly, I can't believe I'd be that insensitive!'

He was good at keeping a straight face but there was a definite twitch to his mouth now. 'Perhaps we'd originally planned to spend it together but you couldn't make it?' he suggested.

'But if I know you're going to be pleased to see me, why book a separate villa?' Thea was beginning to enjoy herself. 'I mean, we *do* sleep together, don't we?' she joked.

Rhys looked across the table at her, his gaze dropping from the wide, quirky mouth to the generous cleavage revealed by her sundress. 'Definitely,' he said and, when he looked back into her eyes, Thea was mortified to find herself blushing.

'That's good,' she said, although not quite as casually as she would have liked. 'I wouldn't want Kate to think that I was no fun.'

'No danger of that,' said Rhys, taking in the wide grey eyes and the mobile mouth that tilted up at the corners and seemed permanently on the point of breaking into a smile.

OK, this was getting silly. Look away from his eyes now, Thea told herself. *Now*, she added urgently and at last managed to jerk her gaze away. This was just a joke, she reminded herself as she tried to get her breathing under control. That was it, inflate the lungs, breathe out…and again…

'Ah, so you just want me for my body?' She tossed her head and the cloudy brown hair tumbled around her face. 'I thought you loved me!'

'I do,' said Rhys. 'Madly. You're the woman I've been waiting my whole life for.'

Thea hated the way he could say things like that and look so *normal*, as if the idea—absurd though it was—wasn't causing little flutters in the pit of his stomach or interfering with the smooth functioning of his lungs at all.

'Then why aren't we sharing a villa, if you love me so much?' she asked almost tartly.

Rhys thought for a moment. 'You've got Clara with you because of your sister's accident and you need more space?'

Thea wrinkled her nose. 'She and Sophie could always share a room,' she pointed out. 'It's not as if the villas are pokey. There's plenty of room for four in ours, and—oh, I've got it!' She held up a hand dramatically, and Rhys lifted an amused eyebrow.

'Go on, then.'

'You've kept me a secret from Sophie so far,' she said slowly, thinking her way through it as she spoke. 'You're not sure how she'll react when she finds out that you've got a girlfriend.'

He nodded encouragingly. 'OK.'

'And I'm a bit fed up with this. If you love me as much as you say you do, why won't you introduce me to Sophie?

She's the most important part of your life, and I want to be part of it too. You keep saying that you don't want to rush things, and you think it's too soon.'

'I'm still a relatively new feature in her life,' said Rhys. 'I probably *would* think it was too soon to introduce another new person into it.'

'Well, there you are. But what you *don't* realise,' Thea went on in the same portentous tone, 'is that I'm sick of the way you're refusing to commit, and now I'm putting on the pressure. I've decided to force the issue by coming out with Clara but, because I'm not quite sure how you're going to react, I've booked a separate villa for us.'

Rhys considered. 'Aren't you afraid I'll be angry?'

'That's a risk I'm prepared to take,' she said solemnly. 'You might be cross, but you can't ignore me. By booking my own villa, I'll be forcing you to introduce me to Sophie, just as a friend initially, but at least then you won't be able to pretend that I don't exist.'

She was getting so into the story by now that she was almost starting to feel resentful at the way Rhys kept shutting her out of his life. 'And with my own villa I won't be crowding you, so you can't be *too* angry. In fact, I've probably planned to be quite independent with Clara once I've made my point.'

Pleased with her own inventiveness, Thea sat back in her chair. 'What do you think?'

Rhys was looking at her with open admiration. 'I think it would convince Kate, and if it would convince her it would convince anybody!'

They both laughed, releasing the tension that had underlain the game, until Thea realised that Rhys had stopped laughing and was looking thoughtful instead, and the chuckle dried in her throat.

'You're not serious?'

CHAPTER THREE

RHYS looked at her for a long moment, and then seemed to shake himself back to reality.

'No, of course not,' he said heartily. 'I couldn't possibly ask you to do something like that.' He leant forward and picked up the jug to refill their glasses. 'Have some more retsina.'

She had probably had enough, thought Thea, watching the golden liquid pouring into her glass. The retsina was probably the reason why she had been sitting there joking about anything quite so silly.

Because it *was* silly, and they hadn't been serious, and she ought to be running a mile from a strange man who would even suggest such a thing. She didn't know anything about Rhys Kingsford, other than what he had chosen to tell her this morning.

But it didn't feel that way. It felt as if she had known him for a very long time. It felt almost as if he had always been part of her life.

They sipped their retsina in silence for a while, both thinking about what a ridiculous idea it was to go to such lengths just to avoid being patronised by a woman who meant nothing to either of them.

But still thinking about it, anyway.

'It would be very embarrassing if Kate and Nick found out that we were pretending, wouldn't it?' said Thea eventually as if carrying on the unspoken conversation between them.

'Probably,' Rhys agreed. 'On the other hand, would it be

as bad as spending the next two weeks finding excuses not to go over to dinner?'

'Or explaining why I'm a sad person without a boyfriend,' said Thea.

There was another silence.

It was Thea who broke it again. 'Do you really think we could convince them?'

'I don't see why not,' he said, considering the matter all over again.

'We'd have to pretend that we were in love,' she said, as if the idea had only just occurred to her.

'Yes,' he agreed.

They glanced at each other and then away.

'But that shouldn't really be a problem, should it?' she reassured herself. 'I mean, they won't expect us to be all over each other, will they? Even if we were a real couple, we wouldn't be sticking our tongues down each other's throats in company.'

'Quite,' said Rhys in a dry voice. He hesitated. 'I might have to put an arm round you occasionally or something, though. Would you mind that?'

Thea managed a careless shrug. 'I ought to be able to manage that,' she said as lightly as she could, but it wasn't easy when his lean, solid body tugged at the corner of her eye and the mere thought of being held against it was enough to give her a severe attack of the flutters.

The truth was, she wouldn't mind at all.

'So what are we saying?' said Rhys at last.

Thea took a deep breath. 'I will if you will,' she said.

'Are you sure?'

'Why not?' She sat up straighter. 'It's just a bit of fun. It's not as if you really do have a girlfriend who would be hurt if she found out... Is it?' she added, hoping that she didn't sound too anxious to have this little point confirmed.

'No,' he said with a wry smile. 'I'm keeping all my attention for Sophie at the moment. What about you? No boyfriend likely to turn up and start acting jealously?'

'No.' Thea shook her head a little sadly. She would have loved to have been able to imagine Harry turning up out of the blue and glowering jealously at Rhys, but jealousy had never been Harry's thing, at least as far as she had been concerned. 'I don't think he'll be doing that.'

Rhys hesitated. 'But there is a boyfriend?'

'I'm not sure.'

'You don't know?' he asked in surprise.

'No. I suspect not, but…no, I'm just not sure.' Thea ran a finger around the rim of her glass, her face sad as she remembered.

'I met Harry a year ago, and fell for him like a ton of bricks. He was a dream come true—incredibly attractive, charming, glamorous…and honest. He told me all about his split with his ex-girlfriend and how close he still felt to her. Isabelle is the complete opposite of me.'

'You met her?'

She shook her head. 'No, but Harry spent most of his time talking about her. She's very pretty and petite, apparently, and she works in the City like him. She's got some high-powered job that means she's constantly under pressure and it doesn't help that she's completely neurotic anyway. That's not what Harry says, of course,' Thea added with a twisted smile. 'He says she's "highly strung."'

'I can see that you might be a relief after someone like that,' said Rhys carefully.

'That's what Harry used to say, but I always felt he secretly thought I was a bit dull after Isabelle's histrionics. According to Harry, it was an amicable split, and they both agreed that they would be free to see other people, but as far as Isabelle was concerned she still had first call on his time. At the first hint of a crisis she'd ring him up and he would drop everything to rush round and sort it out for her.'

Rhys's eyes rested on her averted face. 'That must have been difficult for you.'

'It wasn't easy.' Thea managed a shrug. 'Nell—Clara's mother—thinks Harry is weak and selfish, but I told her she didn't understand. Harry's a kind person. He feels that Isabelle needs him and that he wants to be a good friend to her.'

'What about being a good friend to you?'

She glanced at him. 'Funny, that's what Nell used to say, too!' Heaving her shoulders, she let them slump back. 'Oh, I don't know…I suppose I was prepared to put up with anything as long as Harry came back to me. And he did. He'd tell me that Isabelle was just needy, and that I was the one he loved and, of course, I let myself believe it.'

'So how come you're here now, not sure whether you've got a boyfriend or not?' asked Rhys after a moment.

'We'd booked a holiday together.' It still hurt Thea to think about how much she'd looked forward to that holiday. 'I'd found a perfect little cottage in Provence and it was going to be just the two of us, away from Isabelle, but about a month before we were due to go Harry started to back-pedal, saying he wasn't sure it was good timing and maybe we should think about postponing it.

'It turned out that Isabelle had to have some operation on her foot. It wasn't anything major, and she was just an out-patient at the hospital, but she decided that she needed Harry to feed her cat, water her plants, make her little cups of herbal tea, and generally dance attendance on her.'

Thea blew out her cheeks and pushed the hair away from her face. 'Sorry, that sounds bitchy. I'm sure she didn't choose to have the operation just then, and for all I know it was very uncomfortable for her. It was just the last straw for me.'

'So you told Harry he had to choose between you?'

'More or less.' She hated remembering that awful day, and how heartsick she had been. It had felt as if she were deliberately destroying her only chance at love and that she would never be happy again.

'We had a long talk, Harry and I, and I told him how I felt. Harry said that he felt guilty about being constantly torn between the two of us, and that sometimes he felt smothered, so I suggested that he take some time to think about what he really wanted.'

One of the worst things had been seeing the unmistakable relief that had leapt to Harry's eyes, as if he had been trapped, longing for her to open the door for him.

'Harry agreed that he needed some space, so that's what he's doing, deciding which of us he wants.'

'And in the meantime you're left hanging on, hoping that you might still have a boyfriend, but not sure if you do or not?' Rhys's voice was unusually hard, and Thea glanced at him. What was it to him, anyway?

'The last time I heard from him, he still couldn't make up his mind,' she admitted. 'At least that means I can still hope. I didn't get my holiday in Provence, but then Nell had her accident and asked if I would come out with Clara in her place, so…here I am!'

Rhys was frowning down into his glass again, a muscle beating in his jaw as if he was angry about something, but when he looked up after a few moments, he smiled. 'I'm sorry if it wasn't the holiday you wanted, Thea,' he said, 'but I for one am very glad you're here.'

'I think it's Clara you should be grateful for,' she said, conscious of a dangerous little glow flickering into life inside her.

He shook his head. 'You too,' he said firmly, and the glow spread a little further.

Thea looked around her, at the rickety tables dappled with sunlight through the plane leaves, at the pots of bright flowers and the massively gnarled tree trunk dwarfing them all. The air was warm and full of the tantalising smell of grilling lamb while beyond the shade the light glared and a car tooted in a failed attempt to disrupt the peaceful atmosphere.

'I'm glad I'm here too,' she said. 'It's been good to get away.'

'I'm glad you told me about Harry, as well,' Rhys went on. 'I think it makes things easier in a way.'

'What do you mean?'

'Well…it means that there's no danger of either of us taking the pretence too seriously, doesn't it?' he said, not quite awkwardly, but as if he wasn't entirely sure how she would react.

'Oh. No. Quite.'

And that would explain why that glow was still seeping along her veins and she still had that weird fluttery feeling under her skin at the thought of touching him, wouldn't it, Thea?

'No danger at all,' she said firmly.

Rhys smiled and held out his hand. 'Let's shake on it then.'

Oh, dear, touching him just *wasn't* a good idea at the moment. Why hadn't he suggested drinking to it instead? Chinking glasses would have been fine. Even shaking hands seemed fraught with complications given the confused state her hormones were in right then.

But she couldn't see any way to refuse without looking a complete idiot. Thea eyed his hand as if measuring a jump over an abyss, which was almost what it felt like. All she had to do was lift her own hand, touch palms, curl her fingers around his—*briefly*, remember—and let go. How difficult could that be?

Thea took a deep breath, put her hand in his and yanked it back before he could do anything alarming like squeeze it or hold it for too long or anything at all to prolong the warmth that was tingling up her arm as it was.

Rhys looked a little surprised but picked up his glass. 'Here's to pretence,' he said, toasting her.

Why couldn't he have done that before?

'I'm not sure we've really thought this through,' she injected a note of caution as she resisted the urge to rub her arm where it jangled still from his touch. 'We're going to have to explain to Clara, and Sophie knows quite well that I'm not your girlfriend, even one you've been keeping secret up to now. What will she think?'

'It's impossible to tell with Sophie,' he said wryly. 'I can only try. If she doesn't want to play along, we'll have to leave it. One thing, she won't tell Kate,' he added. 'She can't bear her, and is always embarrassingly rude to her. It's partly Kate's fault,' he said in defence of his daughter. 'She will keep criticizing Sophie's behaviour in front of her and comparing it to her boys'.'

'I would have thought that would just make her worse.'

'It does,' said Rhys with feeling, and then his face lightened. 'Ah, here's our lunch.'

The waiter was bearing down on them, plates stacked up his arm, and Thea's mouth watered at the appetising smell. Clara, attuned to food like her aunt, had already noticed the arrival of the meal and was galloping back across the square, followed by Sophie.

'I'm starving!' she said, flopping down into her chair.

Thea caught Rhys's eye and knew that he was thinking about the huge breakfast they had consumed not so long ago. 'Martindale girls have healthy appetites,' she said.

'So I see,' he said with a smile, and his gaze travelled on to his daughter who was picking up her knife and fork with an enthusiasm Thea guessed was unusual. Her thin little face was flushed, and her eyes were brighter as she tucked into grilled chicken.

Wisely, Rhys refrained from commenting on her improved appetite, but waited until they had finished eating before outlining their plan so casually that Thea could only gape at him with admiration. He made it sound a perfectly reasonable idea that two complete strangers should go to such elaborate lengths just to avoid a tedious neighbour.

Clara certainly didn't have any problems with it. 'Cool,' she said, and her bright eyes sparkled, and her enthusiasm won over Sophie, who was clearly uncertain how to react at first.

'The thing is, you two are in on the secret. You won't have to say or do anything, but we'd need to know that you weren't going to give us away,' said Rhys carefully. 'How would you feel about that?'

'I think it would be fun,' said Clara buoyantly, but then she would. Thea could practically see her calculating opportunities to throw her aunt together with Rhys.

'What about you, Sophie?' he asked. 'Would you mind?'

She shook her head. 'No,' she said. It sounded grudging after Clara's effervescence, but it was a big step for Sophie.

'I think you should be engaged, not just girlfriend-boyfriend,' Clara was saying, oblivious to the way Rhys was looking at his daughter.

Thea frowned her down. 'There's no need to go that far, Clara.'

'But if you're just a girlfriend, this Kate person won't think Rhys is really serious,' Clara protested.

'You know, I think Clara might have a point,' said Rhys, eyeing her niece with respect. 'I wouldn't put it past Kate to keep thinking up potential girlfriends for me in case you turn out not to be suitable after all. What difference does it make, after all? We'll still be pretending.'

'True.' Thea looked from her niece's bright face to Rhys and back again. Really, that girl was going to go far. She was only nine, and already she had manipulation down to a fine art. But she could hardly tell Rhys that she didn't want to pretend to be his fiancée because it might give Clara ideas, could she?

'Oh, well, in for a penny, in for a pound.' She sighed, resigned, and Clara sat back with a smug smile.

'What about a ring, things like that?' To Thea's consternation, Rhys was actually looking to Clara for advice. Didn't he realise that she was only nine, for heaven's sake?

'That won't be necessary,' she intervened quickly before Clara could pronounce. 'We'll just say that you were so thrilled to see me at five o'clock this morning that the scales fell from your eyes. You want to spend the rest of your life with me, and you don't want to waste any more time, so you asked me to marry you there and then.'

'What, at five in the morning?' said Rhys incredulously.

It didn't sound that convincing put like that, Thea had to admit. Would she really want to be proposed to in the early hours after a drive like that without her make-up on? No.

'OK, we got engaged this morning, when you'd had a chance to realise that we really do belong together.'

There was one of those sizzling pauses you couldn't plan in a million years, when Thea's words seemed to echo round the village square, booming back at her. *We belong together.*

Rhys broke it first. 'This is our engagement lunch, then?' he said, and Clara seized her lemonade, playing it for laughs. 'Congratulations!' she said, lifting her glass.

What a little drama queen she was! Thea shook her head

at her, but she and Rhys laughed and chinked their glasses against hers and, after a moment, Sophie lifted her glass too.

'Congratulations!' she said, and when she smiled Thea felt as if she'd conquered Everest.

Another silence threatened, and this time it was Thea who rushed to fill it. 'You know, you could be difficult if you wanted to, Sophie,' she suggested. 'You could pretend to make a big fuss and say you hate me, then that would be a reason for you to go off on your own with your dad.'

'But then I wouldn't be able to play with Clara,' Sophie objected.

'Oh, I don't know. You could be nice to Clara because you feel sorry for her stuck with me all the time. And whenever I come by you could glower and look sulky.' Thea demonstrated by putting on a moody face, and Sophie was surprised into a reluctant giggle.

'I think she'd be pleased if you were her dad's girlfriend,' said Clara loyally. 'Thea's my favourite aunt.'

She turned to Sophie, but Thea could tell that her words were aimed elsewhere. 'It's always fun when she comes round. I wish my dad had married someone like her,' she added, one eye on Rhys. 'My stepmother's really boring. I'm not allowed to make a mess when I'm there, and she never lets me try on any of her make-up or clothes. I could never curl up on a sofa and have a chat with her the way I can with Thea. She makes yummy meals, too, not all low-fat and healthy like my stepmother does.'

Such blatant promotion made Thea cringe. She didn't dare look at Rhys to see how he was taking Clara's transformation into professional matchmaker. Any more of this and she would be negotiating a dowry.

'Yes, well, none of this matters, Clara,' she said hastily. 'We're just pretending here, remember? Sophie doesn't really want me to be her dad's girlfriend.'

'I wouldn't mind,' said Sophie shyly, and Clara shot Thea a triumphant look.

Oh, God, here came another of those awkward pauses. Thea still hadn't risked a glance at Rhys, but she was very conscious of Clara's bright eyes whisking interestedly between them and she rushed into speech before her niece could do anything else to embarrass her.

'We should decide how we met. Kate's bound to ask. What about at a party?'

Rhys looked unconvinced. 'I'm not really a party animal,' he said. 'I'm sure Lynda will have told Kate that. It was one of the things she always used to complain about me.'

'You could have decided to change your life since you've come back to the UK,' Thea pointed out. 'You could say you'd had a personality transformation.'

He made a face. 'I don't think I could carry off being the life and soul of the party, particularly as I've spent the last week trying to convince Kate and Nick how unsociable I am. How about if we met on a blind date? I could have seen your ad in a newspaper and thought you sounded interesting.'

Thea bridled. 'I'm not telling Kate that I've been advertising! She'll think I'm desperate.'

'She's going to think that anyway if you're pursuing me out to Crete.'

'Look, who is it who invented the girlfriend in the first place?' she said crossly. 'I don't mind appearing pushy, but I'm not going to be sad!'

Rhys held his hands up in mock surrender, and she subsided slightly. 'Could we have met through work? That's where most people get together, after all.'

'I don't know. What do you do?'

'Oh, a bit of this and a bit of that, as they say. I'm still waiting to stumble into a career,' said Thea with a sigh.

It must be nice to be able to answer the dreaded What do you do? question with confidence. I'm a doctor. I'm a solicitor. I'm a gardener. I'm in sewage disposal. Anything as long as you sounded like you knew what you were doing with your life.

'I keep changing jobs,' she went on. 'It drives my mother wild! I'm a PA in a public relations company at the moment.' She brightened. 'Maybe we could have been raising the profile of your organisation, or changing the focus of your sales? Or—I know!—the key element of what you do needs re-branding, so of course you needed to talk to my boss but as soon as you laid eyes on me, you knew I was the one and naturally you couldn't concentrate on business after *that* and—' She stopped, seeing Rhys's face. 'What?'

'I was just trying to imagine how you could re-brand rocks.'

'Rocks?' echoed Thea, completely thrown. She had been getting quite carried away there, imagining just how it would have been when he walked into her office and their eyes had met…a bit like the way they had met earlier, in fact.

'I'm a geologist,' Rhys explained. 'I'm interested in rocks that are millions of years old. Geology is the most important thing there is.'

Thea, Clara and Sophie exchanged a look. 'More important than shoes?' asked Thea innocently.

'Or shopping?' added Clara, never one to be left out.

Rhys rose beautifully to the bait. *'Shopping? Shoes?'* he echoed incredulously. 'You can't even begin to compare them! Everything you do, everything you see, everywhere you walk, is shaped by geology,' he argued, roused to passion, Thea was interested to note, by a few rocks. 'How can you understand the world around you if you don't understand how it's made? They ought to teach geology in primary schools. If I had my way—'

He stopped as he saw Thea and Clara giggling as they mimed falling asleep with boredom, closing their eyes and letting their elbows slip off the edge of the table, and he grinned reluctantly.

'OK, so not everybody finds rocks as interesting as I do,' he conceded.

Sophie was watching them with huge eyes. It had obviously never occurred to her that it was possible to tease her formidable father, but when she saw that he was laughing too, she giggled.

Thea judged that it was time to bring them back to the business in hand. 'Well, if geologists are too grand to deal with PR, we'd better fall back on that tried and trusty matchmaking activity, the dinner party. We can say a friend of mine works with a friend of yours or something, and we both ended up at the same dinner.'

Rhys shrugged. 'Sounds reasonable enough to me—and not something Kate can disprove either. She's an intimidating woman, but I'd have thought even she would draw the line at demanding names and addresses.'

'OK, a dinner party it was, then. And naturally, when you talked about rocks and showed me how important they were in my life, I was completely dazzled!'

Rhys acknowledged her mockery with another grin. 'Ah, so it was love at first sight for you, too, was it?'

Thea looked at the old men playing backgammon at the next table and wondered what had happened to the air in her lungs. 'I think it probably was,' she said.

The alarm dragged Thea out of a deep sleep, and for a while she lay utterly still, groggily wondering where she was and why there was bright sunshine outside when her body was telling her it was the middle of the night.

She felt totally disorientated. Vivid images kept coming to her in puzzling flashes, none of which seemed to connect in any way. Clutching the steering wheel as she drove endlessly through the dark—she remembered *that*—but then she had a very clear image of Clara positively smirking as well. Surely not?

Then there was a checked tablecloth and a man's arm and Rhys…*Rhys*!

Thea jerked upright. It was all coming back to her now. Yes, she had had coffee with him, and then they had driven down the mountain together. That had all been fine.

But that ridiculous plan they had concocted… What had she been *thinking* of? The retsina must have gone to her head.

'Oh, *God*!' Thea dragged her hands through her hair. What had she got herself into?

The worst thing was remembering how reasonable it had all seemed at the time. They had talked about it as they drove home with their shopping, the girls giggling in the back seat. They had actually *laughed* about it!

Thea blenched, thinking about it now. Nell would have a fit if she knew that Thea had thrown herself and Nell's precious daughter's lot in with a perfectly strange man for the entire holiday!

She would have to get up and explain that she hadn't been thinking clearly, and that they couldn't possibly go through with it. Rhys had seemed the sensible type. He had probably been having second thoughts himself, Thea reasoned, and as for the girls, well, they could just pretend that it had all been a joke.

How did she get herself into these things? Thea wondered

in despair, as she struggled to disentangle herself from her sheet. She had only been in Crete a matter of hours!

It was very hot still, even in the shady bedroom, and the thought of getting dressed properly was just too much to contemplate on top of all the other disastrous situations she seemed to have got herself involved in. Digging out her favourite sarong, she wrapped it around her. Its soft cotton was cool and comforting against her bare skin.

Tiredness had hit her like a freight train on the way back. One moment she had been gaily chatting away in the front seat—extraordinary how she had seemed to have so much to say to Rhys, considering that she didn't know him from Adam...maybe that had been down to the retsina too—and the next her head had been lolling on to her chest.

It had been all she could do to unpack the shopping and shove most of the contents of the bags into the fridge before collapsing into bed. Clara had opted to keep going in the pool, and now Thea wished that she had done the same. She felt lousy, dopey, disorientated, faintly sick and shivery. It was a bit like having a monumental hangover, but without the headache.

She padded downstairs. Perhaps a swim would freshen her up too. She would just check to see that the dreaded Paines weren't back. She didn't want to face Kate for the first time in a swimsuit. That really would put her at a disadvantage. Opening the front door, she stepped cautiously out on to the terrace.

'Thea!'

Thea nearly leapt out of her skin. Clutching her sarong, she swung round to find herself staring at Rhys and an elegantly-groomed blonde who Thea had no difficulty at all in identifying as Kate Paine.

So, instead of meeting her in a swimsuit, their first encounter had Thea tousled and half-naked in a piece of material so old and worn it was practically see-through. Her eyes were piggy with sleep still, and her hair was its usual tangled mess. Instinctively, Thea lifted a finger and wiped it under her eyes.

It came away black. She had been too tired to take her make-up off when she fell into bed, which meant that she had mascara circles under her eyes and looked like a panda.

Excellent.

Rhys and Kate had evidently met on the terrace and seemed as startled to see Thea as she had been to see them. Why? Thea wondered crossly. It was *her* terrace.

For a moment the three of them just looked at each other, and Thea was just wondering if she could, in fact, simply turn and walk back inside and close the door, when Rhys pulled himself together.

'There you are, darling!' he said, advancing on Thea with a warm smile. He put an arm round her before she could follow her instincts and bolt back inside. 'I was just coming over to see if you were awake yet! How do you feel?'

'A bit odd, to tell you the truth,' said Thea huskily, finding her voice at last.

Ooh, look, she had suddenly turned into the Queen of Understatement. Now that *was* odd. Odd was much too ordinary a word to use for the way it felt to have Rhys's arm around her.

He held her firmly, his arm strong and solid and warm through the fine material of her sarong, and Thea was agonizingly conscious of her nakedness against him. The merest whisper of cotton separated her skin from his, and the thought was peculiarly exciting. It was all very well reminding herself that she hardly knew this man, but the sad truth was that his arm felt…well, *good*. Right, even.

Disturbingly so, in fact.

'I've just been telling Kate how you surprised me last

night,' Rhys said with a warning squeeze which Thea could have done without. Her sarong was in a precarious enough position as it was, not to mention her nerves.

It wasn't even as if she needed reminding of the situation when she was pressed up against his body like this. It felt satisfyingly unyielding. He might not have Harry's glamorous looks, but he was all bone and muscle.

'Remember I mentioned the family staying in the third villa?' he was saying to Thea, as if they hadn't spent their entire lunch working out how they could avoid them as much as possible. 'This is Kate Paine. She's here with her husband, Nick, and their two boys.'

Everything about Kate said cool and crisp. She had icy blue eyes and her hair was both stylish and practical. She radiated the kind of confidence that left Thea feeling the way she had at primary school when faced with a particularly brisk teacher. It was impossible to imagine her ever getting dirty or flustered.

Thea eyed her pristine white shirt and immaculately ironed stone-coloured trousers with disbelief. It would be bad enough to think that Kate had unpacked them looking like that, but Thea was prepared to bet on the much scarier thought that here was someone who not only took an iron on holiday, but used it!

'Hugo and Damian,' Kate was explaining graciously, but her eyes were coolly assessing as they rested on Thea in a return inspection. She didn't look over-impressed.

Thea couldn't blame her. She knew what she looked like when she woke up, and it wasn't a pretty sight.

'Hello,' she said, managing a sickly smile.

'Kate, this is Thea.' Rhys sounded positively adoring, and now he was smiling down into her face as if he thought that she was beautiful instead of ridiculously smeared with mascara.

Who would have thought a geologist could act like that?

'Kate's kindly invited us for drinks on their terrace tonight,' he went on with another of those alarming squeezes.

'Oh, well, that's very kind of you,' Thea began, but Kate interrupted her before she could formulate a decent excuse.

'Just a drink to welcome you,' she insisted. 'Rhys has explained that this is a special day for you, but we *would* like to help you celebrate your engagement as well.'

'Well...'

'I'm sure you'll want a chance to freshen up,' Kate said kindly, although the eyes that inspected Thea from head to toe were unmistakably critical. Clearly the slatternly look held no appeal for her. 'We'll expect you at six, shall we?'

CHAPTER FOUR

'WHY didn't you make some excuse?' muttered Thea as Kate clicked off on her perfectly polished shoes. 'I thought the whole point of the pretence was to avoid them, not spend our time having drinks with them.'

Rhys waited until Kate was out of sight before dropping his arm. Having willed him to do just that, Thea found that she missed its warm support and perversely wished that he would put it back.

'We had to go some time,' he said as she concentrated fiercely on her sarong instead, tying it in such a tight knot that she was in danger of cutting off her circulation altogether.

'We might as well get it over and done with,' he went on. 'I'd rather have waited until tomorrow, but when I saw her heading over here I thought I'd better come and cut her off. I managed to stop her before she got to your door, and told her about our touching little romance. Agreeing to drinks was the best way I could think of to get rid of her. I didn't think you'd want to meet her unprepared.'

'No, really, I'm delighted I could meet her like this instead,' said Thea with more than a touch of sarcasm. She gestured down at her sarong, but carefully. She didn't trust the slippery material. 'With me looking so smart and all!'

Rhys smiled, one of those swift, disturbing smiles of his. 'I didn't know you were going to open the door just then,' he pointed out. 'Anyway, you look great.'

'It's all right,' said Thea, flushing slightly. 'You don't need to act when the Paines aren't here.'

'No, I mean it,' he said.

Uh-oh, here came one of those tingly moments again. Thea didn't want to look at him, but it was as if her eyes had a will of their own, dragging her head round until she was gazing straight at him.

'Really,' he said with a smile.

Oh, please don't do that, Thea wanted to say. She was having enough trouble coping with the peculiar behaviour of her hormones as it was.

She moistened her lips. 'I keep forgetting you've been out in the desert with no women for the last few years,' she said, and he laughed, which just made things worse.

Sighing inwardly, Thea made an effort to pull herself together. Really, it would be much easier if he would just go back to being grumpy and disagreeable, the way he had been when they had first encountered each… Was it only that morning? She felt as if she had known him a lifetime.

'So.' From somewhere she produced a bright smile. 'We're committed now. Kate seemed to believe that we've known each other longer than a few hours.'

'So far, anyway,' Rhys agreed. 'We've still got to get through the inevitable interrogation over drinks, but if we brush through that, we should be fine. I hope they'll leave us to do our own thing after that. Kate wanted us to go over for supper, but I compromised on drinks, the subtext being, I hope, that a quick gin and tonic was all we could manage without ripping our clothes off each other. I thought drinks would be enough to cope with!'

'Quite enough,' said Thea, trying not to imagine the clothes ripping scenario too clearly.

Glancing at her watch, she saw that it was already almost six. 'I was on my way to check on Clara and have a swim, but I think I'd better have a shower now. Have you seen Clara at all?'

'I have. I've been keeping an eye on them all, and it took her about five minutes to subvert the Paine children from good little boys to shouting, splashing and dive-bombing with the best of them,' said Rhys with a grin. 'They're all having a great time, although Kate didn't look too happy with the transformation in her sons.'

'Oh, dear. Do you think I should go and have a word with Clara?'

'No. The other three have been staring at each other all week, and it's taken Clara less than a day to get them all playing together. They'll enjoy the rest of the holiday now. I'd say Clara was more than a match for Kate, anyway!'

Thea laughed. 'You're probably right. I'll go down and see what's going on when I've had my shower.'

'I'll see you at the pool, then, and we can go over to the Paines' together.'

With a wave, Rhys set off down the steps, leaving Thea to wonder why she should feel vaguely resentful, and then to be horrified when she realised that it was because he had gone without kissing her goodbye.

God, she *must* pull herself together! They were pretending, remember? Rhys didn't really want to marry her and he didn't have to kiss her at all, and she shouldn't want him to. She was supposed to be broken-hearted about Harry, anyway.

Turning to go inside, she reassured herself that she was just confused after a long day. She would be fine tomorrow, and in the meantime maybe a shower would help.

Preferably a cold one.

Thea was aghast when she caught sight of herself in the bathroom mirror. With her hair all over the place, a white pasty face, bleary eyes and horrible black mascara smears, she looked as if she had stumbled off the set of a horror movie. *The Afternoon Nap of the Undead* perhaps. No wonder Kate had looked unimpressed!

Clearly drastic measures were called for. Thea jumped into the shower, washed her hair and slathered on the curl control cream. This was no time for restraint on the lotions and potions front.

By the time she had dried her hair it didn't look *too* bad. Still no sleek, shining curtain, but at least it looked more like a fluffy cloud and less like a haystack. It had been worth bringing that hair-dryer after all. Nell had said that she wouldn't need one, and it was nice to know that her big sister could be wrong sometimes.

Glad that there was no Clara this time to ask awkward questions, Thea made up her eyes carefully and pulled on a cherry-red dress. It was one of her favourites, quite old now, but still the most flattering for her curvaceous figure, emphasising her cleavage and drawing attention well away from her hips and thighs. Lovely soft material too, that floated around her bare legs. Wearing it always made her feel sexy.

The only trouble was that it creased badly. Thea tried smoothing down the skirt again, but it didn't make much difference. Still, it would have to do. With any luck it would get dark soon anyway, and she was damned if she was going to ask Kate if she could borrow her iron!

Six o'clock… Thea squinted at her watch. 'OK,' she muttered, scrabbling through her make-up bag for a lipstick. 'Lipstick…lipstick…lipstick…ah, there you are! Now… shoes…earrings…*earrings!*…God, what did I do with my earrings?'

She looked wildly around the room. If only it wasn't in such a mess where she had pulled everything out of the case earlier. She'd never be able to find anything now.

Thea was frantically tipping various cosmetic bags out on

to the bed in search of her jewellery when she suddenly realised that she was hyperventilating, as breathless and excited as if she were going out on a heavy date.

'Calm down,' she told herself and took some deep breaths. It was just drinks with tiresome neighbours.

And supper with Rhys, that sly inner voice whispered.

Yes, well, that too, but really she was dressing to convince Kate that she didn't always look like an extra from *Buffy the Vampire Slayer*, Thea tried to convince herself. All this effort was simply in aid of the pretence.

Sure, said the voice.

It was a bit much when your own inner voices went sarcastic on you, Thea reflected glumly, spotting her earrings at last. They were supposed to restrict themselves to the occasional note of caution, not outright mockery and discomfiture.

Maybe it *did* look as if she had made too much effort for casual drinks, though? Thea's confidence, ever shaky, faltered as she squinted at herself in the bathroom mirror while her nerve got ready to run off and hide in the bushes with its tail between its legs.

Thea bit her lip. There was no time to change now. She was late already. Whistling her nerve to heel once more, she straightened her shoulders. It wasn't as if she was togged up in sequins and a tiara. She was only wearing a dress, for heaven's sake.

'Get a grip,' she said sternly to her reflection.

Judging by the squeals, splashes and giggles emanating from the pool, Clara hadn't spent the afternoon missing the care and sound counsel of an adult, although Thea was relieved to know that Rhys had been keeping an eye on the girls while she had been crashed out in bed.

By rights Clara should have been exhausted too, but no,

there she was, in the thick of it and, by the looks of things, all four of the children were thoroughly over-excited.

Obviously Thea wasn't the only one who thought so. As she came down on to the poolside, she saw Kate, as immaculate as ever but looking exceedingly tight-lipped as she watched a little boy leap off the side of the pool and land with a terrific splash.

'Hugo! Damian!' she was shouting. 'How many times have I told you not to jump in like that? Get out right now!'

'Oh, *Mu-um*...'

Poor kids. Imagine not being allowed to dive-bomb in a private pool on holiday, thought Thea. The Paine household was obviously run as a very tight ship, with instant obedience the norm to judge by their mother's astonishment at being answered back.

'It's after six, boys,' Kate said, careful to sound reasonable, because clearly Kate was the perfect mother who never lost her temper. 'You know perfectly well that you always have a bath now, and then you're ready for the evening.'

'But we're playing this brilliant game,' one of the boys objected.

'Everyone is getting out now, anyway.' Kate's eye fell on Thea. 'Ah, good, there you are,' she said briskly, as if Thea was an errant pupil who had turned up late without a proper excuse. 'You want Clara out now, don't you, Thea?'

Behind Kate's back, Thea could see Clara shaking her head emphatically. 'I don't see why, if she's enjoying herself.'

'But she must be tired!'

'She's on holiday,' said Thea with a touch of defiance, trying to ignore the jubilant thumbs-up signs Clara was making from the pool. 'She can sleep in the morning if she wants.'

Kate sucked in her breath. 'Are you sure that's wise? I

gather Clara is your niece, and it's obviously tempting to be indulgent when it's not your own child,' she added patronisingly, 'but parents know that children really need routines.'

'At home, maybe, but I would have thought that the whole point of a holiday is to give the child a break from routine,' said Thea, ultra-reasonable.

Balked, Kate swung back to the pool. 'Well, the other three are certainly getting out now,' she said crossly. 'I'm sure your father will think *you've* had enough, Sophie.'

'Enough what?'

At the sound of Rhys's voice behind them, Thea's heart leapt into her throat and lodged there, quivering, as she swung round. He had put on a clean shirt and shorts, and he looked crisp and clean and self-assured, but there was nothing special about him. He didn't have Harry's romantically floppy hair or dazzling blue eyes or chiselled features. He was just ordinary, really.

So why did it feel as if every cell in her body had jerked to attention at the sight of him? Why, after knowing him only a matter of hours, did he seem so familiar, and yet so joltingly immediate at the same time?

And why did the way his cheeks creased as he smiled—yes, like that—dry the breath in her throat?

'You look wonderful,' he said, ignoring Kate completely, and slipped an arm around her waist. Before Thea—and possibly he—had quite realised what was happening, he had dropped a warm, casual kiss on her mouth.

Caught unawares, Thea's heart, already in turmoil, seemed to stop altogether. The paving round the pool dropped away beneath her feet, and for a moment she swung dizzily in space, her only anchor the searing, dangerously exciting touch of his lips.

It was just a moment, though. The next Rhys was lifting

his head, and as their eyes met fleetingly, Thea thought he looked as shaken as she felt. It was almost as if he had acted without thinking, and now wasn't sure what had happened.

Kate was tapping her foot impatiently. 'I was suggesting that all the children get out of the pool now and get ready for bed,' she told Rhys, apparently unaware that his arm was all that was keeping Thea upright. 'They're all getting over-excited, and the boys have been in there quite long enough. When they've had their baths, I think they should sit quietly and read so they can all calm down before they go to bed.'

Rhys looked at the children in the pool. 'They don't look to me like they're in much of a mood for reading,' he said.

'That's because they're playing this silly game,' said Kate, exasperated.

'Games are supposed to be silly, aren't they? Isn't that the point of them?'

'The point *is*,' Kate said icily, 'that Sophie isn't usually in the pool this late, is she?'

'Oh, *Dad*,' begged Sophie, who had been hanging around near the edge waiting to hear her fate. 'Don't say I have to go to bed yet! We're playing this totally cool game, and Thea says Clara doesn't have to get out.'

'Hugo and Damian are getting out,' Kate intervened, provoking another chorus of moans from her sons, 'so Clara will get pretty lonely in there on her own.'

Rhys let go of Thea and went over to squat by the edge of the pool so that he could talk to Sophie. 'You can stay in with Clara while we have drink,' he told her, 'but when I call you, I want you both out straight away.'

'Thanks, Dad!' Sophie could hardly believe her luck.

'That goes for you too, Clara.'

'OK.' Clara beamed, and celebrated by doing a handstand

on the bottom of the pool. 'Thanks Rhys, thanks Thea!' she called when she surfaced.

'Rhys.' Kate lowered her voice as he straightened and came back towards her and Thea, whose legs were doing the most amazing impersonation of cotton wool and who was still rooted to the spot where he had left her, afraid to move in case she simply collapsed.

'Are you sure it's wise to give in to her like that?' Kate went on in concern. 'I know Lynda believes in setting very strict boundaries, otherwise Sophie can be, as you know, quite...well, *difficult*...'

'I know all about Lynda's boundaries, thank you, Kate,' said Rhys in a cool voice. 'Lynda's not here, I am responsible for my daughter, and for once she seems to be having a good time. I'm not going to spoil that by insisting on needless confrontation. Now, did someone say something about a drink?' he finished, closing the discussion firmly.

Wow, assertive or what? Thea watched, incredibly impressed, as Kate gave ground. She obviously longed to make an issue of it, but there was something in Rhys's face that evidently made her decide not to push the matter.

'Yes, of course,' she said, forcing a tight smile. 'Nick's waiting for us now.'

Kate's husband was waiting for them at the top of the steps. He was a big, florid man, exuding *bonhomie*. 'Come up, come up,' he urged them, and wrung Thea's hand. 'I'm Nick, Nick Paine. Paine by name, pain by nature!' He laughed heartily.

You said it, thought Thea. What was it about people who laughed at their own jokes that made them so intensely irritating? She had hardly stepped on to the terrace and already her teeth were on edge. No wonder Rhys had been so keen to find a way to avoid them. Thank God she had listened to him, instead of insisting on finding out what the Paines were like for herself. It would have been too late then.

'Thea Martindale,' she replied with a polite smile, extracting her hand with some difficulty from Nick's clammy clasp, an extra incentive, if one was needed, to make her pretend engagement to Rhys as convincing as possible.

'But not for much longer, I gather?' Nick ogled her cleavage. 'That Rhys is a dark horse! He never breathed a word about you, and now Kate tells me that you're getting married!'

'That's right.' Thea stepped back before Nick actually fell down her cleavage and took Rhys's hand, which was warm and strong and dry and infinitely comforting. A contrast to Nick's, in fact. 'We're so happy.'

'We must toast your health.'

Thea sensed that Kate was not overly pleased by this unexpected development. She might be in favour of Rhys getting married again, but only to someone of her choice, and definitely not anyone related to subversive influences around the pool!

Still, to do her justice, she wasn't going to say it outright, however much she might want to.

'Nick, get the wine.' Kate didn't quite snap her fingers, but she might as well have done the way Nick leapt to obey.

Thea sat down next to Rhys on a bench and wondered whether Lynda was like her friend. She couldn't imagine Rhys responding well to a barked order.

'Well, here we here!' Kate waited until Nick had poured out four glasses, and lifted her glass. 'Congratulations!' she said, but smiled in a way that made Thea a little nervous. 'You must tell us everything!'

Ah, the interrogation. 'Have you known each other long?'

'Not long, no,' said Rhys, and Thea quickly trotted out the dinner party story to explain how they had met.

Kate frowned slightly. 'I thought Lynda said that you'd been abroad so long you didn't know anyone in London?' she said. 'She was quite worried about you when you came back.'

'I know these friends who had the dinner party,' said Rhys coolly, 'and of course I know Thea now.'

He rested his hand on the back of the bench and his thumb caressed the nape of Thea's neck, sending delicious shivers down her spine. She would never be able to concentrate if he kept on doing that.

'I'm surprised you're engaged already,' said Kate, disapproving. 'You can hardly know each other.'

'I knew the moment I saw Thea that she was the woman I wanted to spend the rest of my life with,' said Rhys, sounding so convincing that Thea lost track of her breathing for a moment.

And then he lowered his arm from her neck to take her hand instead, lifting it to his mouth and kissing it. 'You don't need time to fall in love, do you, Thea?'

She shook her head dumbly, her fingers curling hopelessly around his. 'No,' she said, but her voice came out as barely more than a croak.

'Have you told Lynda yet?' asked Kate, which Thea thought was a bit tactless of her. On the other hand, if it was her friend, she would probably want to know too.

'No,' said Rhys evenly, 'but I will, of course, when we get home. We only got engaged today,' he explained. 'It was a spur of the moment thing, but it feels absolutely right.'

'I see.' Kate looked between them, an oddly calculating look, and it occurred to Thea that she might not be as convinced by their story as they had hoped.

'We're getting married at Christmas,' she put in, feeling that a few corroborating details were required.

'Christmas is only four months away!'

'I know, but I've always wanted a Christmas wedding,' said Thea disingenuously. 'We'll have plenty of time to organise things. We don't want anything too elaborate, do we, darling?'

She took the opportunity to snuggle closer to Rhys and gaze winsomely up at him. 'Just family and close friends, and of course Sophie and Clara as bridesmaids. It'll be lovely,' she finished with a misty look. She was tempted to heave a sigh as well, but didn't want to overdo it.

'Sure you know what you're doing, Rhys?' On his way round with the bottle to top up their glasses, Nick gave him a nudge that nearly made Rhys spill his wine. 'I'd make the most of my freedom, if I were you! You haven't been back from the desert long, and there are lots of nice girls out there.'

'I don't want a nice girl,' said Rhys. 'I want this one.'

Laying a warm palm against her far cheek, he turned her head until she was facing him, and very gently he touched his mouth to hers. It was a brief, sweet touch, over much too soon.

Rhys drew back and for a moment they just looked at each other, before leaning towards each other once more, their lips moving as if they had a will of their own, catching and clinging with a kind of desperation. Nick and Kate were forgotten as they kissed, and that strange glow that had been simmering inside Thea since she had seen Rhys smile for the first time ignited with a whoosh, spilling fire along her veins.

The feeling was so intense that when Rhys broke the kiss once more, it was all she could do not to grab him back to her and make him kiss her again. But he was sitting back, saying something to Nick and apparently carrying on the conversation as if nothing had happened at all.

How did he *do* that? It was taking everything Thea had not to slide off the bench into a puddle on the terrace. She was quivering inside and out, and her pulse was booming so loudly in her ears that she could hardly hear a thing. It was only when she realised that the other three were looking at her curiously that she realised that she was being asked a question.

'Sorry?' she said huskily.

'I was just asking what you do.' Kate's perfectly shaped brows rose slightly, as if in faint surprise that Rhys should have chosen someone apparently incapable of following a simple conversation.

'Oh…I…er…I'm a secretary.' Thank God Kate hadn't asked her anything more difficult.

'A *secretary*?' Kate echoed as if she had said something extraordinary.

'Yes. Well, a PA, really. In a PR firm.'

'Oh.' Kate was clearly deeply unimpressed. She glanced at Rhys. 'Thea is obviously very different from Lynda!'

'She is indeed.' Rhys put his arm around Thea once more and met Kate's eyes squarely. 'Very different.'

Kate didn't seem to think that the point had been adequately made. 'Lynda was a lawyer when I first met her,' she told Thea. 'She's gone on to start up her own business. She's a marvel, isn't she, Rhys?'

'She certainly seems to have become very successful,' he said, non-committal.

'And you're just a secretary.' Kate sighed, turning back to Thea. 'It *does* seem a waste,' she lamented. 'I mean, you seem quite intelligent, Thea. Haven't you ever thought about a proper career?'

'What sort of thing did you have in mind?' asked Thea, who was finding it hard to concentrate on what Kate was saying. She was burningly conscious of the strong arm around her and longing to turn her face into Rhys's shoulder, to burrow into him.

'Oh, you know,' said Kate. 'A solicitor, for instance.'

'I can't quite see myself as a lawyer,' Thea confessed. 'I'm not very ambitious, I'm afraid. To be honest, I'd be just as happy having children and looking after a home. We're planning a big family, aren't we?' she added to Rhys.

'At least four children,' he agreed solemnly.

Kate pursed her lips. 'What about Sophie?'

'Sophie will be part of the family,' said Thea, meeting Kate's disapproving eyes, her own very clear and direct. 'Of course she will.'

Thea and Clara had breakfast on their own terrace the next morning. They had their own coffee, their own yoghurt and honey, their own peaches, but somehow none of it tasted quite as good as it had the day before.

It wasn't the same without Rhys and Sophie. They had agreed the night before that they shouldn't feel obliged to spend all their time together and that was good, naturally, but it was as if the light was less bright this morning, her appetite less sharp, the sounds and scents drifting in the air less intense.

Clara felt it too. 'Can I go and see if Sophie wants to play?' she asked as soon as she had finished her peach.

'OK. I'll be down in a minute,' said Thea and then, as Clara skipped off, she added, 'Oh, if you see Rhys, tell him I'm going to spend the day by the pool, so I'll keep an eye on Sophie if he wants to go out.'

There, that sounded perfectly natural, as if she didn't really care whether she saw him or not. As if she hadn't spent hours lying in bed last night remembering those kisses and reliving the way they had sat talking on the terrace after supper, listening to the cicadas rasping frantically in the dark.

They hadn't got round to cooking a proper meal. Rhys had barbecued some lamb and Thea made a salad, and afterwards the girls disappeared. Sitting side by side, feet up on the low terrace wall, Thea hadn't been touching Rhys, but she'd been agonisingly aware of him, of his lean, solid strength, of the line of his jaw, of the gleam of his eyes when he'd turned his head to look at her.

He was nothing special, she kept telling herself. There was no reason for her pulse to kick whenever he smiled. She was just on the rebound from Harry.

Yes, that was it. Harry's departure to think about things had left an emptiness in her life and now she was subconsciously casting around for someone to fill it. Rhys simply happened to be the first man who had swum into her orbit.

Of course, there had been Neil at work, who had asked her out several times so, strictly speaking, Rhys wasn't quite the first...or the second, now she came to think of it. She'd forgotten about Andy from the flat downstairs, who was always offering to sort out her CD player for her. Both would have been ideal rebound material, now Thea came to think of it. She hadn't felt like this about either of them.

Thea had picked a piece of mint from the pot on the terrace and rubbed it between her fingers, enjoying the smell even as she tried to justify her unaccountable attraction for Rhys to herself.

So she wasn't desperate... Well, that was a good thing, wasn't it? Maybe it was more a question of timing? She was alone and on holiday and the normal conventions didn't apply. It was the classic scenario for a holiday romance, in fact. You fancied yourself attracted to someone quite different but you weren't committed to anything, because you both knew that at the end of two weeks you'd say goodbye, so you could relax and have your confidence boosted by having a good time with no strings attached.

It made sense, Thea had thought, lifting the mint to her nose and feeling better. Of course, with Clara and Sophie around, there was no question of embarking on a fling with Rhys, but at least now she could explain her own peculiar reactions to herself.

So now she could relax and stop feeling guilty and confused about the way Rhys made her feel, right?

Thea had studied Rhys under her lashes. He was pointing at the velvet blue sky, and telling her about the stars in the desert, his face animated, and she had felt something shift deep inside her as she'd watched him.

Yeah, right.

Now Thea gazed down at the pool, glinting in the bright morning sunshine. Clara and Sophie were already there, sitting on the edge and dangling their feet in the turquoise water, their heads bent together as if they hadn't spent most of the night before talking.

She would see Rhys again today. He might come to the pool and, even if he didn't, she owed him dinner. Thea smiled and stretched luxuriously. The day stretched lazily ahead of her, with absolutely nothing to do but try and convince him that she wasn't quite such an idiot as Kate had made her appear. She might not be a dynamic businesswoman, but she too could be cool, calm and in control.

Today was the perfect opportunity to christen her new swimsuit. Sadly, bikinis and her figure didn't go together, but she had found a one-piece that was really quite flattering if she held her tummy in and lay very still.

When Rhys found her, she was draped decoratively over one of the sun loungers by the pool, one leg oh-so-casually bent to avoid splayed thigh syndrome, and apparently absorbed in the book Nell had lent her. According to the cover, it had been short-listed for several literary prizes, and Nell had raved about it.

'You *must* read it, Thea,' she had insisted, and Thea had judged it easier to pack it rather than protest that she would be much happier with a rollicking blockbuster. Now she was pleased that she had. The book lent her a certain *gravitas*, she felt, and she had secreted a couple of glossy magazines under the lounger for later when no one was looking.

'Good morning, Thea.'

Thea lifted her sunglasses and squinted up at Rhys. 'Oh...hi.'

Her voice was a bit squeaky, but otherwise she didn't think it sounded too bad for someone whose heart had just done an elaborate series of somersaults. The way it did when you were cool and calm and in control.

He sat down on the edge of the lounger beside her. 'You look very comfortable.'

'I am. I'm planning a lazy day to recover from all yesterday's excitements.'

Rhys twisted his head round to read the title of her book. 'Are you enjoying that?'

'It's marvellous,' said Thea, who hadn't a clue what was going on, and had been stuck on the same page for at least half an hour. She didn't understand why books like this had to be such hard work, but she was glad now that she hadn't succumbed to the lure of *Marie Claire*. It wouldn't do Rhys any harm to see that even secretaries could engage in literary discussion before lunch.

'Have you read it?' she asked him, mentally crossing her fingers, and hoping devoutly that he hadn't. If he wanted an in-depth analysis of the plot, she'd be sunk. Fortunately, he was a scientist. Chances were that he didn't go in for any arty-farty stuff like this.

But Rhys was nodding. Really, why couldn't he conform to his stereotype? Thea wondered crossly.

'I thought it was rubbish,' he said. 'You're obviously more intellectual than I am. I didn't understand a word of it.'

Phew! Thea beamed at him in relief. 'Well, I've only just started it,' she said, settling her glasses back on her nose. 'I might persevere with it for a while. I haven't got anything else to do all day, so if you wanted to go off and do anything on your own, here's your chance.'

Translation: here's your chance to say that you'd rather stay here with me.

'Are you sure? Clara did mention that you were happy to keep an eye on Sophie, and there is a walk that I've wanted to do for some time. It's too long for Sophie, though, so this might be an opportunity.'

So much for the seductive effect of her swimsuit, Thea thought glumly. He couldn't wait to get away. Perhaps she had intimidated him by seeming too intellectual. That would be a first, anyway!

'I feel a bit guilty, though,' Rhys was confiding. 'I should really be spending time with Sophie, not leaping at the chance to go off on my own.'

He sounded so unsure of himself that Thea put the book aside and sat up to reassure him. 'You have been spending time with her,' she pointed out. 'What you should be doing is letting her have a good time, and she is. Look at her now.'

Rhys followed her gaze to where Sophie and Clara were hanging off a lilo and chatting animatedly as they drifted around the pool.

'She's transformed,' he agreed. 'Normally she converses in monosyllables, but she was positively chatty at breakfast this morning. I don't know how to thank you,' he added, and the expression in his eyes made Thea's throat tighten.

'It's nothing to do with me,' she told him. 'Thank Clara.'

He looked back at the pool. 'I will,' he said.

CHAPTER FIVE

THERE was a tiny silence, and then Rhys got to his feet. 'Will you be all right having Sophie for the day?' he asked, looking down at Thea, who put on a martyred air.

'It'll be a terrible struggle lying here in the sun all day—' she sighed '—but I expect I'll cope somehow.'

Rhys laughed and got up from the lounger. Walking over to the pool, he hunkered down to have a word with Sophie. Behind her glasses, Thea admired his back view. Not many British men could carry off shorts that well, but Rhys had just the right lean, brown, I-spend-my-life-squinting-at-far-horizons look about him.

Clara was splashing over to talk to Rhys, hauling herself up to fold her arms on the edge of the pool and dangle there while she carried on an animated conversation with him, punctuated by giggles from both girls.

'What was all that about?' Thea asked as Rhys straightened and headed back to her with an odd expression on his face.

He didn't answer directly, nodding down at her lounger instead. 'May I?'

'Sure.' A little surprised, Thea shifted her legs over so that he could sit down, and put down her book again.

It felt very intimate to have him so close. He was sitting facing her, so that her arm was very close to his bare knees and her legs were almost touching his thigh.

Her heart had started that slow, painful thumping that interfered with her breathing again, and she was very glad of the sunglasses that hid most of her expression, which otherwise would be a dead giveaway. Without them she might as well have *kiss me, kiss me!* emblazoned on her forehead.

That was it, Thea, cool, calm and in control!

She swallowed hard. 'If Clara was putting in a plea for an ice-cream run later, we've got a whole tub in the freezer.'

'No,' said Rhys slowly, 'it was a little bit more delicate than that.'

'What?' God, it was hard to concentrate when her entire body was jangling with the awareness of how close his hand was and how easily he could smooth it along her thigh.

'She was pointing out that Kate was making a poor job of pretending not to watch us from her terrace.'

Thea lowered her sunglasses and glanced surreptitiously over the rim to the Paines' terrace, where Kate was indeed sitting at the table where she had a perfect view of what was going on at the pool.

'You can hardly go over and tell her to stop looking,' she pointed out. 'It's her terrace. She can sit where she wants, surely.'

'That's not quite what Clara had in mind.' There was a thread of amusement in Rhys's voice that made Thea look at him suspiciously.

'Oh? What exactly *does* Clara have in mind?'

'She thinks it would be a very good idea if I kissed you goodbye.'

'Oh...' The breath leaked out of Thea's lungs and she couldn't get it back, especially when Rhys smiled quizzically.

'She seems to be taking the whole pretence very seriously!'

That was because Clara was determined to turn pretence into reality, thought Thea, but she had better not tell Rhys that.

'I know.' Her answering smile was decidedly nervous. 'I think it's something to do with having a vivid imagination. I wonder where she gets her ideas from sometimes. Television, I suppose. Nell's always complaining that she watches too many soaps.'

Oh, great, now she was babbling. Rhys was talking about kissing her, and all she could do was witter on about television. Thea took a deep breath and made herself shut up.

'So what do you think?' asked Rhys after a tiny pause, presumably to check that she wasn't going to start drivelling on about something else.

'Um…about a goodbye kiss?'

'Yes.'

'Well, I…I suppose it wouldn't do any harm. I wasn't sure Kate was entirely convinced last night.'

'That's what I thought.'

Another silence, longer this time. Long enough for Thea to wonder if he could actually hear her pulse booming.

'We'd better make it look good, then,' said Rhys.

'Might as well.'

Thea was mortified to hear her voice disappear into a squeak. 'Let's give it a go,' she tried again. That was better—casual, relaxed, no big deal. This wasn't about getting involved, it was about feeling good and keeping it light.

The trouble was that it didn't feel light. It felt dangerous and disturbing as Rhys leant forward, very slowly. She could change her mind if she wanted to, but now his hand was on her thigh, warm and firm, and her heart was slamming against her ribs, making it hard to breathe and even harder to think.

Deep inside her, anticipation churned, quivering out to the ends of her fingers and the tips of her toes, but all at once he was hesitating. Don't say he had changed *his* mind?

It was too much for Thea. As if of their own accord, her

hands lifted to his arms, sliding upwards to wind around his neck and pull him towards her, or maybe she didn't need to pull him, maybe Rhys was closing the distance between them anyway. But, however it happened, they were kissing at last and the release from all that anticipation was so intense that Thea gasped in spite of herself.

His lips were so tantalising, the hand smoothing over her thigh so warm and so sure, it was enough to make a girl forget what she was doing. Thea certainly forgot to think, forgot anything but the sheer pleasure of kissing and being kissed, of being able to touch him at last, run her hands over his back and savour the feel of his hard, strong body.

Fortunately, Rhys had himself under better control, or who knew where it would have ended? He pulled back slightly to look down into her face with an expression Thea couldn't quite identify.

'Very good, Thea,' he said.

'Just getting into my part,' she said a little unsteadily, and Rhys smiled.

'You're a natural.' Reaching out, he stroked a finger down her cheek in a gesture so tender it dried the breath in Thea's throat, and then got to his feet. 'I'd better go. See you later, girls,' he called as he headed off to his villa.

'Bye!' they yelled, as if nothing unusual had happened at all and it was perfectly normal for him to kiss Thea and then get up and walk off.

Thea was just grateful that she was already lying down and didn't have to try and walk anywhere. She was quite sure that her legs wouldn't have held her if she had been upright. It was bad enough trying to behave normally as it was, with this shaky feeling and that odd jittery sensation under her skin.

So much for calm, cool and in control.

Across the pool, she saw Clara wave and make a cheeky

thumbs-up sign. Really, that girl was too clever for her own good, thought Thea, shaking her head back at her. She would have a word with Nell about her when she got home.

Picking up her book with hands that trembled slightly, she tried to read, but the words were dancing in front of her eyes. How could she be expected to concentrate on impenetrable prose when her lips were still tingling from that kiss, when her thigh was burning where he had touched her?

Her whole body was pulsating. This was ridiculous, Thea scolded herself. It was only a kiss. She was completely over-reacting, as usual. Hadn't she decided last night that she was just suffering the symptoms of a holiday romance, and that there wouldn't be a problem if she could keep things light-hearted?

Thea laid her fingers against her skin where his hand had been, and squirmed at the memory. For a light-hearted romance, it sure felt very intense. That kiss had been wonderful—warm and exciting and, if she was honest with herself, much, much too short.

And just a pretence. Don't forget that bit, Thea.

To hell with this stupid book! She had been staring at the same page for what felt like days. Tossing it aside, Thea leant under her lounger and pulled out one of her magazines instead. She was never going to stop thinking about Rhys and that kiss when she didn't understand half the words on the page. What she needed now was a distraction. The new look on the catwalk, the latest mascara, a little celebrity gossip and she would soon regain her equilibrium.

As it turned out, this was an excellent idea, and Thea was absorbed in the marital difficulties of two of Hollywood's biggest stars when a shadow fell over her. Kate was standing there, perfect eyebrows oh-so-slightly lifted as she checked out Thea's reading matter.

Oops, how not to impress Kate! Kate was clearly much

too clever to waste her time with magazines, let alone gossip. Quickly, Thea flicked over the page. She could at least pretend to be stuck into one of the more serious articles about women's issues, but found herself instead staring at a headline trumpeting 'Sex that makes *you* look slim and *him* feel huge!'

Perhaps she should show Kate the article and they could have a girlish giggle together about it? Or perhaps not, Thea decided, glancing at the immaculate Kate with her air of efficient sophistication. Kate just wasn't the type for a giggle.

With an inward sigh, Thea closed the magazine altogether, but made a mental note to go back to it. She was always up for a laugh, and she would try anything that promised to make her look slimmer without the hassle of dieting or going to the gym.

'Do you mind if I join you?' asked Kate, dropping her bag on to the next lounger without waiting for Thea's answer.

Well, what could she say? 'Of course not.'

Kate was wearing a sarong, just as Thea had the day before, but where Thea's had kept slipping and falling apart, Kate's was elegantly and securely tied. Now she was unwrapping it to reveal a perfectly tanned and toned body in the kind of bikini Thea could only ever dream of wearing.

The kind of bikini that might have been specifically designed to make Thea feel fat and blowsy. Give her some whiskers and a couple of tusks, and she'd be a dead ringer for those great, blubbery walruses you saw floundering around the beach in their rolls of fat on nature programmes, she thought glumly. It was amazing to think that she had been quite pleased with her appearance earlier.

She eyed Kate with resentment. Look at her, not even having to hold her stomach in as she sat and oiled herself complacently, perfectly aware of the contrast her trim, taut figure made with Thea's voluptuous curves.

If only her mother hadn't brought her up to be so polite, Thea could have moved to the other side of the pool, or preferably taken that tube of suntan lotion and squeezed it all over Kate's shiny blonde hair. As it was, she was stuck feeling fat and inadequate and making polite conversation.

'Where are Damian and Hugo today? I was expecting to see them in the pool with the girls.'

'Nick's taken them to the archaeological museum in Heraklion.'

'Gosh, won't they be bored?'

'Certainly not,' said Kate crisply. 'They're both very interested in history. Hugo's a member of the local archaeological society. He's got his own trowel.'

Thea laughed until she realised that Kate was not being humorous. Should have known better, she thought with an inward sigh.

'It's so important that children learn something about the culture of the country they're staying in,' Kate was saying. 'I'm sure you agree.'

'Oh, yes, absolutely,' said Thea, who couldn't be bothered to argue. She amused herself instead imagining Clara's reaction if she suggested that she might like to forgo a day in the pool to go to a museum.

Kate settled herself on the lounger. 'Is Rhys not joining you today?' she asked delicately, as if she hadn't been watching him say goodbye to Thea from her observation post on her terrace.

'He's gone for a hike,' said Thea, conscious of a warm little thrill down her spine at the mere memory of how he had said goodbye.

'I think it's marvellous of you not to mind him going off on his own on your first day here.'

Thea looked at her sharply. It was hard to tell whether Kate took her seriously or not. In the end, she managed a careless shrug.

'I'm feeling lazy, and you know Rhys. He's not one for sitting around.' At least, she didn't know whether he was or not, but he hadn't struck her as a man who would be very interested in sunbathing, and it was a fairly safe bet that Kate wouldn't know either.

To her surprise, Kate took this very seriously. 'Yes, I gathered from Lynda that Rhys has problems relaxing.'

'I didn't say that,' said Thea, unaccountably annoyed. 'Just that he didn't like sunbathing.'

'Nick and I think it's marvellous Rhys has met someone at last,' Kate confided earnestly. 'I know Lynda was quite worried about him for a while. She was afraid he was never going to get over her leaving. She's often said to me that she knows how much damage she did to him, and she feels very guilty about that.' Kate leant towards Thea. 'Apparently he was absolutely devastated when she left. He absolutely adored her.'

'Really?' said Thea discouragingly.

She didn't want to hear about Rhys from Kate, and she certainly didn't want to hear about how much he loved Lynda, and frankly she thought it was monumentally tactless for Kate to assume that she would. As far as she knew they really were engaged, after all.

Picking up her magazine, she opened it once more in the hope that Kate would take the hint, but the woman clearly had the hide of a rhinoceros.

'No, Lynda says that he never really seemed to accept that she had left for good,' Kate went on in the same concerned tone. 'She really wanted him to be able to move on, but of course the first thing he did when he got back to

London was to buy a house just around the corner from Lynda.'

'It's possible that he wanted to be near his daughter, not Lynda,' Thea was provoked into saying, and Kate nodded as if she had made an interesting point. Wrong, but interesting.

'That's what Lynda hoped, but I think she was secretly afraid that he was trying to be part of her life again. It wouldn't be surprising if he did. Lynda is a beautiful woman and very talented. It's an old-fashioned word,' she went on, oblivious to Thea's unreceptive attitude, 'but I always think that Lynda is really *accomplished*.'

'Really?' said Thea coldly again.

The chill in her voice was lost on Kate, who was still burbling on about Rhys's ex-wife. 'Did you know that she set up her own business selling alternative therapies? They're absolutely marvellous and we all swear by them!'

Kate's cold blue eyes swept over Thea. 'I'm sure she'd have something that could help you lose weight,' she added as an aside and then swept on while Thea was still open-mouthed at her rudeness and spluttering for a retort.

'She only started it up two or three years ago, but the turnover last year was phenomenal, apparently.' Kate shook her head admiringly. 'She really is a fantastic person—very astute, extremely successful, amazingly insightful... I can't think of anything she isn't good at, in fact. Really, she could make a success of anything she put her mind to.'

Pity she didn't try making her marriage work in that case, thought Thea, fed up with hearing about how marvellous Lynda was. If she was that clever, why were Rhys and Sophie out here on their own?

'Well, perhaps hearing about our engagement will put Lynda's mind at rest about Rhys,' she said acidly, but sarcasm was evidently wasted on Kate too.

'Oh, yes, I'm sure it will,' she agreed. 'She'll be delighted.'

Flexing her toes, she smiled patronisingly at Thea. 'Here's me chatting on, and you want to get back to your magazine. I should have brought something down to read myself.'

'Here, you can borrow this if you want.' Thea fished Nell's book out from under her lounger and offered it to Kate.

Kate's face changed as she saw it. 'Oh, you've got *that*? I hear it's marvellous.' It was obvious that she hadn't expected Thea to be able to read books without pictures in them. 'Lynda's read it twice and told me I should read it. She said it was one of the best books she'd ever read.'

'I think it's rubbish.' Thea smiled sweetly as she quoted Rhys. 'You're welcome to it.'

Defiantly, Thea went back to her celebrity scandal, too cross with Kate by then to care what she thought of her. The other woman had no business gossiping about Rhys's affairs anyway, and that Lynda seemed to take an unhealthy interest in her ex-husband's affairs.

Thea wished Kate hadn't told her anything. Especially, she wished she didn't know how heartbroken Rhys had been when Lynda left. He must have loved her a lot—but then, he seemed to Thea the kind of man who wouldn't get married unless he did love deeply.

Thea turned a page morosely. She couldn't get into the article any more. She had been enjoying it, too, she thought, shooting Kate a resentful glance. It was all her fault.

Be honest, Thea told herself. You don't like the idea of Rhys being in love with anyone else at all.

It shouldn't matter to her one way or another. It wasn't as if there was anything between them. Their relationship was entirely imaginary, and if Rhys was as obsessed with his ex-wife as Kate had implied, it would be better if it stayed that way. Thea had had enough of playing second fiddle to the ex with Harry, and if there was one thing she had learnt, it was that you couldn't compete with emotional history.

Time to stop flirting with the idea of a holiday romance, she decided a little sadly. That would be the sensible thing to do.

It was late afternoon before Rhys returned. Thea was doing her nails in the shade by the pool, and when she saw him she quickly whipped the emery board and polish into her bag. She might have decided not to get too involved, but she didn't want him thinking that she was hopelessly superficial either, even if she was.

She would just have to stick with the natural look for the next two weeks. Lynda was probably far too busy being successful and talented and insightful to do her nails, unless of course she had someone to do them for her. Thea's eyes narrowed at the thought. She sounded like the kind of person who had a weekly manicure. Thea was beginning to dislike her intensely on principle.

Rhys lifted a hand as he saw her, and Thea's heart did a silly little lift of its own in return. Stop it, she told herself firmly, and forced herself to stop smiling quite so widely.

He was on his way round the pool to join her when Sophie called out to him. 'Dad! Dad! Look at this!'

Even from the other side of the pool, Thea could see the blaze of expression in Rhys's face as his daughter demanded his attention, and he stopped to watch her perform a handstand, legs flailing wildly above water for a moment before she surfaced, gasping and spluttering and looking extremely pleased with herself.

'Did you see?'

'I certainly did. I'm impressed! When did you learn to do that?'

'Today. Clara taught me.'

'Have you had a good time, then?'

'Yes.'

Sophie's burst of volubility was evidently over. She went back to practising handstands, and Rhys carried on round the pool to Thea, trying—unsuccessfully—to disguise how moved he was by the brief, tentative connection he was making with his daughter at last.

He was looking hot and dusty after walking all day, but his smile as he sat down beside Thea illuminated his whole face, and she wouldn't have been able to prevent herself smiling back at him even if she had wanted to.

'How was your walk?'

'Hot,' said Rhys, swinging his legs up on to the lounger and leaning back with the contented sigh of someone who had put in a hard day's physical exertion and is entitled to put his feet up. 'Good, though.'

'Lots of interesting rocks, then?'

It was easier to tease him than to think about how much she wanted to be able to go over and sit next to him, the way he had sat next to her that morning, and press her lips to the pulse in his neck below his ear. To kiss her way up his throat and along his jaw to his mouth, to kiss him hello the way they had kissed goodbye earlier.

'Fascinating,' said Rhys. 'I found some great samples of igneous rock. I brought them back to show Sophie and Clara, in fact. I'm sure they'd be interested to know about Crete's ancient volcanic landscape, so I've prepared a short talk. I thought perhaps after supper?'

It took a little while for his words to filter through, and there was a short delay before Thea found herself jolted out of her fantasy of kissing him. He had planned *what*?

'Er, are you sure that's a good idea?'

'Why not?' Rhys met her startled gaze blandly until he gave in and grinned at her expression. 'Don't worry, I'm joking! I wouldn't do that to them, even if they didn't have the attention spans of gnats.'

Lying back, he put his hands behind his head. 'Have they been in that pool all day? They must be completely waterlogged!'

'Pretty much,' said Thea, cross with herself for falling for his teasing, but glad in a way that he had made her laugh. It had released some of the tension of meeting for the first time since that kiss. 'I made them get out for a couple of hours in the middle of the day, and we had lunch in the shade, but they're real water babies, both of them.'

'I didn't realise Sophie liked swimming so much.' Rhys sounded a little sad, as if it was something he should have known about his daughter. 'She didn't spend so much time in the pool last week.'

'I don't think it's swimming so much as splashing around and chatting,' said Thea reassuringly. 'She just needed a friend to do that with, and if there's one thing Clara can do, it's chat!

'Tell me about your walk, anyway,' she went on, trying to keep the conversation on safe ground. 'What was there to see apart from those extremely interesting rocks you mentioned?'

'I went up into the White Mountains and followed a gorge down again. It's wild country, but beautiful.' He glanced at her. 'You should come with me some time. I'm sure you would like it.'

Thea, whose plans hadn't included venturing any further than the poolside, thought about spending the day on a wild hillside, alone with the heat and the light and the drifting scent of wild herbs.

And Rhys.

Something turned over inside her at the thought. 'Maybe I will.'

Her eyes met his then slid away, and there was a pause. 'Well...I'm glad you had a good time.'

'Yes, I did,' said Rhys slowly, 'but, funnily enough, not as much as I expected to.'

'Oh?'

He looked at her, and even in the shade his eyes seemed very light and clear in his brown face. 'It sounds strange, but I missed you.'

'Oh,' she said again, but this time her throat was so tight that she could barely manage a croak. So much for dispersing the tension. The memory of how they had kissed was back with a vengeance, resonating in the air, drumming along Thea's veins, so vivid that Thea couldn't believe that Rhys couldn't feel it too.

But he was looking at the pool, frowning slightly as his gaze rested on Sophie and Clara. 'And the girls,' he was saying. 'It's odd. Most of my work is very solitary, so I'm used to spending a lot of time on my own, and it's never been a problem before, but today I found myself thinking about you all, wondering what you were doing...wishing I was with you.'

He looked back to meet Thea's eyes. 'In the end I took the quicker route back.'

Thea swallowed and reminded herself fiercely about not getting too involved. 'I missed you too,' she said as lightly as she could. 'I had to deal with Kate on my own!'

'Oh, dear.' Rhys grimaced sympathetically. 'Did it go all right?'

'I didn't have to talk much, which was something. She was very keen to tell me how pleased Lynda will be to hear about our engagement. Apparently she has been very worried by you being on your own.'

He made a sound somewhere between a snort and a sniff. 'Kate's quite an authority on my relationship with Lynda, isn't she?' he said sardonically. 'She spent most of the first week telling me how worried Lynda was about my failings as a father.

'I don't spend enough time with Sophie, it turns out, and when I do see her I give her the wrong things to eat, read her the wrong stories, buy her the wrong presents, and let her watch the wrong programmes on television. Basically, I'm the wrong father,' he went on, unable to keep the bitterness from his voice. 'Kate thinks I'm compounding the error of being an absent father by trying too hard, which is probably true.'

'Maybe,' said Thea, 'but it's not up to Kate to tell you what kind of father you should and shouldn't be.'

'Oh, she wasn't saying anything I haven't heard plenty of times from Lynda.' He sighed. 'I missed a whole chunk of Sophie's childhood. I don't know her the way Lynda does.'

'No, but then I gather it wasn't you who left and took Sophie away so you couldn't see her regularly,' Thea pointed out calmly.

'No,' he admitted, 'but I still feel guilty about the missing years. Lynda was right about one thing. I should have been prepared to give up my job in North Africa. Effectively, I put my career ahead of my daughter.'

Having a wife laying down ultimatums about choosing between them couldn't have helped either, thought Thea.

'Could you have got a job in the UK?'

'Not then—or not doing the same thing, anyway.' He lifted his shoulders. 'The fact is that I enjoy my job, and I was involved in what seemed to me an important project. I didn't feel that I could just give up on it—but that doesn't justify the fact that I didn't,' he added quickly.

'It's a good reason for Lynda coming to a compromise, though,' said Thea, and he rubbed his face wearily, his smile a little twisted.

'Lynda doesn't do compromise. She's a very strong-minded woman, and once she decides what's going to happen, that's what happens. She didn't want to live in North Africa any longer, so she left. It was an obvious decision from her point of view.'

He sounded frustrated rather than heartbroken by Lynda's behaviour, Thea couldn't help noticing. Maybe he hadn't been quite as devastated as Kate had made out. On the other hand, it *was* five years ago. He might have got over it, no matter what Lynda wanted to think.

'Lynda wanted a divorce so she could start afresh,' said Rhys, 'and, although I thought about moving back to London the next year so I could share in looking after Sophie, I found myself in the absurd situation where the only way I could pay Lynda the maintenance she wanted while she was setting up her business was to continue working overseas.

'It was only this year that Lynda's business took off and I found a position at a comparable salary so that I can live in London and support Sophie, but now I'm afraid it may be too late. I've missed so much time with her.'

'I don't think you should worry too much,' said Thea comfortingly. 'You haven't been back long and Sophie will come round in time. You saw what she was like just now.'

He wouldn't look at her. 'She's just enjoying herself because Clara is there.'

'Partly, but she was also looking for you. She's been waiting for you to come back so that she could show you that she had learnt how to do handstands. It's the little things that are important,' she told him. 'You can't expect her to turn into a daddy's girl overnight.'

'No, I suppose not.' Rhys sighed in spite of himself.

'Kate was right about one thing, at least,' said Thea gently. 'You *don't* need to try so hard with Sophie. You're her father and she loves you because of that. She just doesn't know how to show it at the moment. All you need to do is be yourself, and let her know that you love her, however sulky and badly behaved she is.'

His face relaxed into a smile. 'You sound very wise for someone who doesn't actually have any children.'

'Oh, I'm an experienced armchair parent,' she told him with a sigh. 'I'm an armchair divorcee too, come to that. You wouldn't believe the crises I've been through with my sister and friends. I've seen it all before!'

'Well, I wish you'd been here at the beginning of the holiday,' said Rhys. 'You might have saved me a difficult week.'

'It's never too late for advice from Auntie Thea,' she said smugly. 'And if I *had* been here last week, we'd have all arrived together and we would have been in Kate and Nick's clutches before we had a chance to concoct some elaborate pretence to get out of seeing them, so you could say it's all worked out for the best!'

He looked at her, sitting comfortably on her lounger, her face glowing from a day in the sun and her hair tumbling in its habitual disorder to her shoulders. She had taken her sunglasses off in the shade, and her grey eyes were warm, the humorous mouth tilted in a smile.

'I'm beginning to think it has,' he said.

CHAPTER SIX

RHYS turned his gaze back to the White Mountains where he had been walking, leaving Thea to wonder just what he had meant by *that*.

'You're good with children.' He returned to the earlier part of the conversation after a while. 'Would you like children of your own?'

'Oh, yes.' Thea sighed a little. 'I'd really like that big family I told Kate and Nick we were going to have, but it takes two, doesn't it? There's not much chance of it at the moment, and I'm not getting any younger either.'

She brooded silently on the matter for a few moments. 'Sometimes I can't help thinking that it would all have been so much easier if my parents had just arranged a marriage for me!'

'Who would they have chosen for you?' asked Rhys, amused.

Absently, she picked a leaf off the geranium beside her and twirled it under her nose as she considered.

'My mother would have picked a man with a nice steady job,' she decided eventually, 'and my father wouldn't have cared as long as he played cricket, so I'd have ended up with a braying, bat-toting accountant in white flannels. I'd probably have been very happy,' she added glumly.

Rhys lifted disbelieving brows and Thea sighed again.

'Or not,' she conceded. 'Of course I don't just want children. I want to spend my life with someone I love and who loves me, someone who makes me laugh and likes me the way I am. Someone who'll stand by me in good times and in bad and won't mind if my hair's a mess or if I put on a couple of extra pounds. Is that too much to ask?'

'It's too much to expect without a lot of hard work,' said Rhys slowly. 'It's not too much to dream about and to aim for, no.'

'I'm always being told I'm a hopeless romantic,' said Thea, shredding the leaf between her fingers. 'Maybe I am. I decided a long time ago that I didn't want to compromise. I always thought that if you wanted everything to be perfect, you should hang out for the right man...but then you find what you think is the right man and it turns out not to be so perfect after all,' she finished, and let the last pieces of leaf drift sadly to the ground.

'I'm sure it will work out for you, Thea.' Rhys sat up and put his feet down so that he could face her. 'I can't imagine Harry won't realise how special you are. If I were in his shoes, I would be on the first plane out here I could find. He might even be on his way now.'

'He doesn't know I'm in Crete,' she said, not meeting his eyes, not wanting to see the kindness and the sincerity and the complete lack of jealousy there.

'Your sister knows, doesn't she?'

She nodded reluctantly. 'Nell doesn't like Harry, though.'

'If Harry could convince her that all he wanted to do was to make you happy, I bet she'd tell him the address anyway,' said Rhys stoutly. 'And if he had any sense he'd be out here now, on his knees and begging you to forgive him and take him back. I know I would.'

Thea smiled a little sadly. She couldn't imagine Harry on his knees to anyone—with the exception of Isabelle, of course.

'The thing is, Rhys, Harry's not like you.'

His face changed. 'No, I know. I'm sorry,' he said heavily. 'I didn't mean to sound as if I was criticising Harry.

He's the one you love, and sometimes there's no accounting for why we love the people who hurt us the most.'

Thea wondered if he was thinking about Lynda, who had hurt him so badly. He looked so solid, so sharply defined in the light. She couldn't imagine how anyone could leave him.

'No, there isn't,' she agreed.

'It doesn't stop you loving them, though, does it?'

She stared down at her hands, all at once desperate to remember how much she loved Harry, but all she could see was Rhys, his light eyes and his strong jaw and his cool, cool mouth.

'No,' she said, feeling suddenly uncertain, as if the ground was sliding away beneath her.

'Don't look like that, Thea.' Rhys put out an involuntary hand and took hold of hers. 'Don't give up hope. Maybe not knowing where you are will make Harry realise how much he misses you.'

That was what Thea had hoped when she left England, but now it was hard to imagine Harry even noticing that she was gone, hard to think about anything when Rhys's fingers were warm and strong and infinitely reassuring around hers.

'Maybe.'

'Look, why don't we do something all together tomorrow?' Rhys released her hand and sat back, and she tried not to mind too much.

'Sure.' It was definitely time to lighten the atmosphere, and she produced a bright smile. 'We could go to the archaeological museum like Hugo and Damian!'

He quirked an eyebrow at her. 'Are you going to try asking the girls if they'd like to do that, or will I have to do it?'

'I think I'll save my breath,' she admitted. 'Where were you thinking of?'

'Knossos. It's a bit of a drive from here, but then so is everything, and you can't come to Crete and not see one of the oldest and most important archaeological sites in the world.'

That was what Nell had said, too. Thea remembered her reply. 'Clara and I won't be visiting any boring old ruins, Nell. We'll be at the pool, or in the shops, and that's the limit of our cultural activities this holiday!'

Somehow the idea was a lot more appealing now that Rhys had suggested it. It would be good for the girls, Thea justified her change of mind to herself. They couldn't spend their whole time swimming and, if they weren't careful, Clara would end up monopolising Sophie and Rhys would hardly get to see his daughter at all. At least if they all went, he would get to spend some time with her.

And if it meant that Thea spent more time with him, well, that was just incidental.

'That sounds great,' she said. 'Always providing we can get the girls out of the pool!'

Rhys put the idea to them over supper. 'Thea's keen to go,' he finished, and Thea shot a warning look at Clara, who knew perfectly well that the words Thea and keen rarely coincided in the context of visiting ruins.

But Clara had evidently not forgotten her plans to distract Thea from Harry and throw her together with Rhys instead. When Rhys asked if she would like to go, she was enthusiastic and carried poor Sophie along in her wake, offering the ultimate accolade.

'Cool.'

In the event, Thea found Knossos much more interesting than she had expected. She couldn't make much sense of the labyrinth of stone steps and passageways, or the higgledy-piggledy collection of palace rooms and tiny storerooms, but there was no doubt that the place had an atmosphere. Just thinking about how old it was made her feel dizzy.

Although that might also have had something to do with the fact that Rhys was beside her, very real and very solid and somehow very immediate amongst the old, old stones.

He steered them away from the crowds of tourists to the quiet parts of the ruined palace in the shade of the pine trees, and he told the girls the story of Theseus and the Minotaur, complete with the kind of blood-curdling detail that had even the streetwise Clara saucer-eyed.

'You mean all that happened *here*?' she asked, and Sophie moved closer to her father.

'The monster's not here any more, is it?'

'No,' he said, putting an arm round her, and she let him draw her into the security of his body as he looked around him. 'They're all long gone.'

'Tell us another story,' she said.

It was very hot, even in the shade. Thea was acutely aware of her surroundings. The air was full of the scent of pine needles, and the cicadas sawed in a deafening chorus. She let Rhys's voice roll over her, feeling the warm, ancient stones beneath her palms, and it was as if all the confusion and the uncertainty and the anguish she had felt since Harry had left was draining slowly but steadily out of her until she was quite empty, and then she was filling up again with a feeling she didn't recognise, but which left her strangely restored.

Her gaze rested on Rhys. After Harry's passion and volatility, he was so restrained, so self-contained, so at ease with himself and where he was and what he was doing. What did it take to rouse a man like him to passion—apart from igneous rocks, of course?

Thea closed her eyes and let herself imagine what it would be like if there was no pretence. No Paines, no Lynda lurking in the background, no Clara watching everything with interest, not even Sophie. If there were just the two of them, and a wide white bed, like the ones in the villas.

Would he pull her down on to the crisp sheets? Would his hands be slow and tantalising, or hard and demanding? Would he smile against her skin, and oh! how would it feel to be able to touch him properly, to wrap her arms around him and let her lips drift over that taut brown body?

The image was so vivid, the desire clenching at the base of her spine so intense, that Thea took a sharp intake of breath and opened her eyes wide to find Rhys and the two girls staring at her in concern.

'Thea?' said Rhys cautiously. 'Are you OK?'

Dizzy and disorientated, struggling against the vertiginous tug of her fantasy, Thea blinked and swallowed hard. 'Yes...yes, I was just...'

Thinking about you kissing me. About kissing you back. About making love.

'...just...um...'

Her voice trailed off, her mind so full of imagining what it would have been like that she couldn't think of a single thing that she might legitimately have been thinking about. In the end, she gave up and she stared dumbly back at him and wondered what it was about someone so ordinary-looking that had her aching with desire like this.

Even Harry, the love of her life, had never made her feel *this*, this raw, physical longing. With Harry, it had almost been enough to be with him, and let the dazzle of his presence envelop her. She had never quite believed that she wasn't dreaming when she was with him.

She had never experienced this piercing desire before, this feeling that if she couldn't reach out and touch Rhys, if she couldn't press her lips to his throat, if he didn't pull her into his arms and lay her down in the dust and the pine needles right there and then she would simply shatter into a million pieces.

The feeling was so intense that Thea was shaken, almost scared. Her mouth was dry and she felt giddy, almost ill. She closed her eyes again in the desperate hope that when she opened them again everything would be back to normal.

'You don't look well,' said Rhys. 'It is quite hot. Perhaps we'd better just sit here in the shade for a while.'

That was it, the heat! She really *was* ill, thought Thea with relief, and she drew a deep breath.

'Do you feel faint? Put your head between your knees.'

It was easier to pretend than to explain, and anyway, she did feel dizzy. Thea dropped her head obediently and Rhys put a comforting hand on her back. She could feel the imprint of his palm burning through the thin material of her dress.

'Better?' he asked after a while.

Thea nodded and straightened slowly. 'I'm fine,' she said, although not with any degree of certainty. 'I don't know what came over me.'

'It's easy to underestimate the heat.'

After studying her with narrowed eyes, Rhys took his hand away at last. Thea wasn't sure whether to be relieved or disappointed. Not that it made much difference, in any case. She could still feel her back tingling where his palm had pressed into her. If she took her dress off, she was sure they would find a perfect imprint of his hand on her skin. They could probably take his fingerprints off it.

'Where are the girls?'

'They've found some kittens,' said Rhys in a resigned tone, and nodded over to a corner of the ruins where Clara and Sophie were crouched down and cooing 'oh…so cute' in a kind of harmony. 'The cats will be wild and probably covered in fleas, but try telling those two that!'

'Oh, well, the fleas won't stand much of a chance. Clara and Sophie spend so much time in the pool any flea will drown in no time.'

'Unless they pass them on to Hugo and Damian first. Then we'll be unpopular!'

Thea laughed and felt better. 'I'm sure no flea would dare to jump on to a Paine. Kate just wouldn't have it. The flea would be sent packing and told that kind of behaviour just wasn't acceptable!'

'You know, you're a very restful person to be with,' said Rhys unexpectedly.

'Me?' She was taken aback. 'Am I?'

'Most of the women I know—like Kate, or Lynda come to that—would be ordering the girls to leave the kittens alone. They'd be worrying about them picking up some nasty disease, and insisting that they did a complete tour of the site with the guide instead, and then organising lunch and fretting about what time we'd need to leave…'

He smiled at Thea. 'I can't tell you how much easier it is to come here with someone like you. You don't worry about any of those things, or if you do, you keep it to yourself. You seem happy just to sit and absorb the atmosphere.'

'I think that just means I'm lazy,' said Thea with a rueful smile. 'That's what Harry used to say, anyway.'

He had used to say that a lot, she realised now she came to think about it. And he had hated the way she dressed. He was always trying to make her smarter, to get her to have her eyebrows shaped, and her hair highlighted. To look more like Isabelle, in fact. Why hadn't she realised that before?

'Restful sounds better than lazy, doesn't it?' said Rhys. 'Restful, relaxing, easygoing…calm…'

Calm? Calm was the last thing Thea felt when she was near him.

'Placid, boring, dull,' she offered instead.

Rhys shook his head at her as he got up. 'Thea Martindale, your self-confidence needs a lot of work!' He held out a hand to help her to her feet. 'I think you'd better stick with me until we can do something about that negative image you have of yourself.'

Thea looked at his hand for a moment before she took it and felt the by now familiar thrill run up her arm and settle with a shiver of pleasure deep inside her. And the equally familiar pang as he let her go.

'I think I better had,' she said.

Afterwards, looking back, Thea was amazed at how little time it took them to fall into a routine. The days drifted timelessly by. Whenever she thought about them later, each one seemed to be drenched in sunlight and permeated with the smell of thyme and dust, with cicadas whirring and clicking in the background.

If it had been up to them, Sophie and Clara would have spent every minute in the pool, but they usually let themselves be persuaded to go out, on condition that they could swim when they got back. It took several days of badgering for Rhys to get them to consider a walk and, after much grumbling and groaning, they agreed.

'Just to shut you up,' warned Thea, but actually, once she was out there, she loved it.

They walked along the bottom of the gorge, overhung by trees which provided cool shade splashed by patches of bright sunlight. The river bed was dry, and the girls clambered over boulders and dabbled their fingers in the occasional pool of water that remained, and forgot to moan about the fact that the batteries had run out in Clara's portable CD player.

Another day, Rhys took them up into the mountains and

they had a picnic on a rocky hillside, observed incuriously by a flock of goats. Careless of the dust, Thea lay back in the fragrant scrub and looked up at Rhys's profile, outlined against the deep blue sky.

In the crystalline light, she could see the lines around his eyes and the first few grey hairs at his temple. She could see the texture of his skin, the crease in his cheek and the hint of stubble along his strong jaw, and when he turned his head to smile down at her, his eyes were warm and light.

'Are you comfortable down there?' he asked.

'Very comfortable,' said Thea, fighting the same vertiginous feeling that had swept over her at Knossos. At least this time she was lying down. If she closed her eyes, she would swear that she could feel the earth turning slowly beneath her.

It got harder and harder to remember Harry and how desperately unhappy she had been when he left and she had put her life on hold while he took the time to sort out how he really felt.

Much, much harder, too, to remember everything that she had decided about not getting involved with Rhys. Occasionally, Thea would remind herself that time was passing, even if it didn't feel like it. The holiday would come to an end, and when these two weeks were over there would be no reason to pretend any more. No long, lazy days, no starlit nights on the terrace, just the two of them, while inside the girls gossiped and giggled.

No Rhys.

They talked easily, like old friends. Rhys talked about Sophie and about his determination to be a good father. He told Thea about his job and what it was like to stand on a dune in the middle of the Sahara and turn three hundred and sixty degrees and see nothing but sand and sky. He tried to explain his fascination for rocks, and she tried to explain her fascination for shoes. They laughed a lot, and they talked about everything really.

Everything except what would happen when the holiday ended.

Thea always shied away from thinking about that, and she would put it firmly out of her mind. How could she think about leaving when the sun was shining and Rhys was waiting for her on the terrace? She was afraid of thinking beyond the here and now, and of spoiling what they had.

Not that they 'had' anything. They might pretend to be lovers when they saw Kate or Nick at the pool, but they were just friends. There was no question of them being anything else with Sophie and Clara there in any case, and no indication that Rhys was even thinking about it. Thea told herself that it was just as well, and that friendship was enough.

Only it wasn't, not really.

Rhys preferred to be out in the wild hills, but he was outnumbered by the girls and Thea, who liked the beach best, so he gave in with good grace and drove them down to the coast whenever they asked. They had a favourite beach, on a curving bay where the waves rolled gently in and sighed against the sand, and the sea was a deep turquoise colour and the water so clear that you could see the tiny fish that nibbled your toes if you dawdled too long in the shallows.

Clara and Sophie would run past them, shrieking, and throw themselves into the deep water, diving into the waves like seals. Thea would rather have liked to do the same, but didn't think it would look very dignified.

They were there again towards the end of the second week, although Thea was in denial about the fact that they had only a couple of days left and refusing to even think about it. She stood on the edge of the water with Rhys, watching the girls dash in past the fish, and remembered the sharp little bite she had got last time instead.

'Come on, let's go in too,' said Rhys and set off, only to stop when he realised that Thea was still safely on dry sand. 'Aren't you coming?' he asked, apparently unbothered by the fact that the fish might be swarming towards him like mini piranhas even then.

'Yes,' said Thea, but she hesitated. She wished she hadn't started thinking about swarming fish and their potential for a feeding frenzy.

'Don't tell me you're scared of a few little fish, too!'

'Certainly not.' She put up her chin, and then dropped it as she met his amused gaze. 'Well, not much, anyway. They can give you a very nasty nip, you know.'

Rhys laughed and splashed back through the shallows. Before Thea had realised what he had in mind, he had scooped her up and was heading back into the sea.

Instinctively linking her arms around his neck, she was torn between laughter and embarrassment and the excruciating awareness of his body against hers. His arm was under her knees, hers around his powerful shoulders and the meeting of bare skin was like an electric shock.

He carried her out to where the sand shelved away and paused. Thea thought that he was going to drop her in, and braced herself for the splash, tightening her arms around his neck.

'Don't,' she begged, half breathless, half laughing.

'Don't what?' he said, laughing down into her face.

'Don't throw me in. Please,' she added, clutching him with a mock imploring look. 'I'll do anything!'

'Anything?'

'Yes! I promise!'

Rhys's smile faded. 'I'll remember that,' he said, and

Thea's own laughter evaporated along with the last of her breath as she found her eyes locked with his.

Very slowly, without taking his eyes from her face, he took his arm out from under her knees so that she slid down his body until her feet touched the bottom. They stood very close, her arms still wound around his neck, his hands strong and warm against her back, as the sea rocked gently around them, lapping Thea's waist.

She stood stock-still, afraid to move in case he let her go. *Kiss me*, she willed him as his eyes darkened. *Kiss me now.* She knew that he wanted to, she could see it in his face, but of course he couldn't kiss her, not here, not now, with the girls swimming over to join them.

But later, on the dark terrace, when the girls were asleep…he might kiss her then.

Please, please, please let him kiss her then.

As Sophie and Clara splashed up, Rhys let her go at last and turned to the girls, listening to them clamour for him to pick them up and throw them into the waves. Rather shakily, Thea swam further out to sea, well out of splash range, and floated on her back for a while as she tried to calm her thunderous pulse and the insistent booming of her body.

The waves rose and fell gently beneath her as they rolled into the shore, and Thea faced up to the truth at last. Being friends was not enough. She wanted him, ached for him, *needed* him. The sea was cool, like silk against her body, but she felt as if it should be steaming and sizzling around her, as she thought about running her hands over his shoulders, down his back, all over him, about feeling his skin against her, his mouth on her…

Desperately, Thea rolled over and trod water. She wished she could be like Sophie and Clara, who could clamber over him like puppies. She could hear their squeals of delight as

Rhys swung them round and round before launching them into the deep water.

He was standing sturdily, his body braced to keep them safe. There was nothing obvious about him—ever—but he was toughly-built, strong yet contained and, to Thea right then, irresistible.

She could see the water droplets gleaming on his back and the wonderful sleek line of his shoulders. The sunlight on the water threw a rocking pattern of reflections over his skin, and his muscles rippled as he lifted Clara high in the air and tossed her into a wave. Sophie was already jumping beside him, wanting her turn again.

Lucky girls, thought Thea wistfully. They could keep the being thrown into the water bit, although that was obviously the highlight for them. All she wanted was to be held against him, to slide her arms around him and taste the salt on his skin.

All right, stop it now, Thea, she told herself sternly. She was getting carried away. This was just lust, a purely physical thing. Maybe she was seeing him in his swimming shorts too often? It was hard to avoid noticing that lean, strong body when you were on the beach. If she only ever saw him in a suit and tie, she probably wouldn't be getting into this state.

But things were no better when they were dressed once more and she was sitting next to him in the car. In long trousers and a short-sleeved shirt, Rhys could hardly be accused of flaunting his body, and she still wanted to crawl over him, to press herself against him and feel his hands unlock her.

This was awful. Thea linked her fingers desperately together in her lap to stop them reaching out for him. If only Rhys would give some indication that he was feeling the same tug of attraction, she would feel better. At least then she might look forward to being alone with him later.

But, apart from that one moment when he had let her slide down his body and held her in the sea while he looked in her eyes, Rhys was behaving with intimidating normality.

He put the key in the ignition but didn't switch it on, glancing at his watch instead and turning in his seat so that he could look at her and at the girls in the back seat at the same time.

'It's half past four,' he said. 'We don't need to go back just yet. Why don't we go on to Agios Nikolaos and have a look around there? It's a nice old port. Maybe we could have some supper too? We're having drinks with the Paines tomorrow night, so this is our last chance for a farewell bash.'

'Will there be shops?' asked Clara, leaning forward so that she could cross her arms on the back of his seat and focusing on essentials.

'Lots, I should think.'

'Good. I need to buy a present for Mum.'

Sophie had brightened as well. 'I've got some money left, too. We could go shopping.'

'Thea?'

Thea was still flinching from his casual reference to a farewell supper. Could they really only have one more day?

She forced a smile. 'Shopping sounds good to me.'

'And there was me thinking you'd be more interested in the restaurants,' said Rhys, putting the car into gear. 'Let me buy you a slap-up meal, anyway!'

Well, here was a turn up for the books. She, Thea Martindale, wasn't hungry! She must have it bad if she had lost her appetite, Thea tried to joke herself out of it, but she couldn't get rid of that sick little feeling that came with knowing that very soon she was going to have to say goodbye.

Agios Nikolaos was a bustling port, with ferries, cruise ships and gaily painted fishing boats jostling in the harbour, restaurants ranged along the waterfront and, to the girls' delight, plenty of shops. It was early evening when they got there, and the town was bathed in a golden light as they wandered around.

Clara must have been into almost every shop before she was satisfied with a present for Nell, while Sophie gave the choice of a fridge magnet the same kind of attention Thea would a mortgage. More, probably.

Since she was there, Thea took the opportunity to buy a few presents, too, and told herself that shopping made her feel better. If she could only find a decent shoe shop, she would be almost herself again.

Rhys bore it all with commendable patience and finally managed to drag them away from the shops. They found a restaurant overlooking the small inner harbour where it was quieter, and the girls sat down long enough to compare their purchases over a Coke before they were itching to be off again.

'I suppose it's too much to expect you to sit still and converse nicely until the food arrives?' said Thea, resigned.

'Oh, please say we can, Thea!' Clara wheedled, hugging her from behind. 'We won't go far.'

'We might as well let them go,' said Rhys. 'They'll just fidget otherwise.'

'Thanks, Dad. Come on, Clara,' said Sophie quickly, and the two of them ran off to explore before Thea could raise any further objections.

That left Thea alone with Rhys and unable to think of a single thing to say. Paralysed by a new kind of shyness, she concentrated on pulling a piece of bread apart and on trying to keep her eyes from crawling all over him.

She was excruciatingly aware of him, of the strong brown forearm resting easily on the tablecloth, of the fingers that curled around his glass. Of the broad wrist and the firm jaw and his mouth, especially his mouth. Her entire body was tense with the need to reach across the table and touch him, to remind herself that he was here and real, to store up the memory of how he felt before he was gone.

Her tongue felt as if it was stuck to the roof of her mouth as the silence stretched unbearably, but Rhys was unperturbed by it. He had pushed his chair back slightly so that he could watch the hustle and bustle around the harbour, and he looked utterly relaxed.

Utterly unconcerned by the fact that they would be going their separate ways very soon.

'I'd forgotten we'd agreed to have drinks with the Paines tomorrow.' Her voice sounded horribly stilted, but at least she had broken the awful silence. 'I didn't realise that would be our last night.'

'Neither did I when Kate suggested it,' Rhys admitted, 'but she seemed so keen on meeting up that it was hard to say no. After all, we've got out of seeing them very successfully over the last couple of weeks.'

'I suppose it won't kill us to go and be pleasant for an hour or two,' Thea agreed. 'I just hope Clara behaves herself. Kate's not at all charmed by her. It's obvious she thinks that Clara is a subversive influence around the pool.'

'Yes, I've noticed Hugo and Damian have been a lot less well-behaved since your niece took charge of activities!'

Thea couldn't help laughing, but that was a mistake. Their eyes met as he smiled, and the conversation promptly dried up once more.

Damn, and she had been doing so well sounding normal there for a while!

'Dad!' Fortunately Sophie was back, hanging off Rhys's chair. 'Dad, have you got two euros? We need two coins.'

'What on earth for?'

'We want to have a go on the Mouth of Truth.' Sophie gestured across to where Clara was waiting impatiently beside a stone mask set into the wall. 'It's a hand analyser,' she explained. 'It reads your palm and you get a computer printout that tells you your fortune, and you can choose if it's in Greek or English.'

'Oh, well, that'll be worth the money then,' said Rhys with a sigh. 'You do realise, don't you, Sophie, that this printout will just be a random sample of total nonsense?'

'Yes, yes…' His daughter nodded, shifting from foot to foot, evidently not listening to a word. 'But can we have a go?'

Rolling his eyes, Rhys dug in his pocket for two coins while Thea suppressed a smile, glad to have been distracted from that terrible tension. It was such a pleasure to see how Sophie had blossomed over the two weeks, she reflected. She had filled out, and now had a lovely golden glow to her, and her relationship with her father was transformed beyond recognition.

The girls were soon back, bearing sheets of computer printout. Sophie thrust hers at Rhys. 'Can you read mine for me, Dad?'

Rhys sighed and fished the glasses he wore for reading and driving out of his shirt pocket. He settled them on his nose, looking over the rims at the girls with mock exasperation, and that was when it hit Thea.

There was an extraordinary moment of utter stillness, as if the world had simply stopped. The wooden boats rocking in the harbour, the boys on their skateboards, the waiter weaving his way through the tables, even Clara and Sophie waiting eagerly to hear what the printout said...all froze and faded in Thea's consciousness, until there was just Rhys.

Just Rhys and the sudden certainty that she was completely, hopelessly and utterly in love with him.

CHAPTER SEVEN

SO IT was Rhys. How about that?

Rhys. With one peculiarly detached part of her mind, Thea was astounded. It had been odd enough when she had thought that wanting this ordinary-looking man with his slightly greying hair and his reading glasses and his passion for rocks was a purely physical thing.

And now she had to face the fact that it was so much more than that.

She had never felt this before—this sense of recognition, of utter certainty that he was the one, the man she could love for the rest of her life. There he was, peering over his glasses, the only man who could make her happy, and, odd or not, no one else would do.

It was an amazing feeling. Thea felt her heart swell and lift with the simple relief of being able to look at him, to think *I love you* and be absolutely sure. She shook her head slightly with a kind of dazed and joyful disbelief. All he had done was to put his glasses on, and this had happened!

Thea looked slowly around, expecting everything to be different and was unable to understand why it wasn't. The world hadn't stopped at all. The boys were still showing off on their skateboards, the boats still rocked gently on their moorings, the waiter had deposited a bottle on the next table and disappeared back into the kitchen. Clara and Sophie were listening avidly to Rhys.

Not one of them realised that her life had changed completely in a single instant and would never be the same again.

'"You sometimes feel dissatisfied by everything,"' Rhys finished reading Sophie's printout, '"but you will have a long and happy life." So that's all right then.' He put down the piece of paper. 'What does yours say, Clara?'

Clara smoothed the paper out on the table in front of her while Rhys took off his glasses and glanced across at Thea with a smile that turned her bones to water.

'Let's see if the Mouth of Truth can get to grips with Clara!'

'"You could be seriously disappointed by rash ventures,"' Clara read out loud. '"You are full of vitality and physical pleasures."' Her face changed as she read the next line. '"Beware of trying to be too clever,"' she read with an outraged expression, only to grin reluctantly when she saw the others laughing. 'Stupid thing.'

'I'm beginning to think there might be something in this hand analyser after all!' said Rhys.

'You have a go, Dad!'

'Yes, go on, Rhys,' urged Clara. 'You too, Thea!'

In the end it was easier to give in. Resigned, Rhys found another couple of coins, and they inserted their hands in the hole in the wall, feeling decidedly foolish.

'I'll read yours if you like, Thea,' Clara offered when they were back at the table.

Her eyes scanned the page. 'OK…the Mouth of Truth says that you are a very kind and loving person—that's true, isn't it?' She looked up triumphantly. 'You see, it *does* work!'

'Sure,' said Thea, rolling her eyes. 'What else does it say?'

'Um…you have good health but you often look for love in the wrong place. Well, that means Harry, of course!'

'Who's Harry?' asked Sophie, puzzled.

'Thea's boyfriend. He's awful.' Clara made a face. 'He

looks all right and he says all the right things, but you just *know* he doesn't mean them.'

She hadn't noticed Thea's expression, but Rhys had. 'Read mine, Clara,' he said quickly.

'Oh...OK.' Diverted, Clara took his printout and prepared to read. 'The Mouth of Truth says that you are a per... per...a *perfectionist*,' she said carefully after a whispered consultation with Thea. 'With a sometimes obsessive attention to detail. Does that sound right?'

'It's not too far off the mark,' he admitted grudgingly.

'Oh, and listen to this!' Clara looked up excitedly to make sure she had all their attention before she read the next prediction. 'One of those rare, brilliant marriages which often happens to the really fortunate seems to lie in store.'

'That shows how much the Mouth of Truth knows then, doesn't it?' said Rhys. 'Funny that it didn't know I'm divorced if it's so clever!'

'It could mean a second marriage,' said Clara and Sophie nodded.

'Maybe it means when you marry Thea, Dad.'

There was a tiny pause.

'Thea and I aren't getting married, Sophie,' said Rhys carefully after a moment. 'We were just pretending when we told the Paines that we were engaged.'

'Oh, yes. I keep forgetting.'

Rhys didn't so much as glance at Thea.

'It's easy to do,' he reassured his daughter. 'Sometimes I do it myself!'

'Can Sophie sleep over?' Clara begged when they got back to the villa later that evening.

'I don't know, Clara,' said Thea doubtfully. 'It's quite late already.'

'But it's our last chance! Rhys says we won't be able to

do it tomorrow night because we're leaving so early the next morning and we have to pack.'

It was her last chance to talk to Rhys, too, thought Thea. Once the girls were in bed she would be alone with him, and she could tell him about that incredible moment of revelation on the harbourside that evening, when he had put on his glasses and she had fallen in love.

Quite how she was going to do that, Thea wasn't sure yet, but she would think of something. After all, she had seen the expression in his eyes when he carried her out into the sea, and he had told Sophie that he forgot they were only pretending to be engaged sometimes, hadn't he?

Of course that *might* have been a joke, just to make Sophie feel better. Thea's confidence, ever fragile, faltered and began to trickle away. There hadn't been so much as a flicker of a meaningful glance since then, had there? No accidental brush of the fingers, no murmured aside that he must talk to her soon, and now it sounded as if he was planning an orderly departure with no fuss and no emotions.

Having persuaded her aunt to agree, Clara danced off to convey the good news to Sophie, and a few minutes later the two girls reappeared, accompanied by Rhys, who was carrying Sophie's bedding.

'Just on the off-chance they'll stop talking long enough to go to sleep,' he said.

Thea kissed the girls goodnight and left Rhys to give them a stern five minute warning. 'I don't suppose they'll take much notice,' he said in a resigned voice as he came downstairs.

'You can get heavy-handed with the discipline when you get home,' said Thea. Having longed for the time when they would be alone together, she felt incredibly nervous now that it had come. 'They're still on holiday.' She swallowed. 'So are we. I think we should all make the most of it.'

There, could there be a better cue than that? *Let me make the most of it by taking you in my arms and kissing you until you tell me you love me and want to spend the rest of your life with me.* That was all Rhys had to say now.

He didn't, of course.

'I expect you're right,' he said instead, sounding tired and not in the least romantic. He rubbed his face wearily.

'It's been a long day,' said Thea. 'Come and have a drink and relax.'

Rhys followed her out on to the terrace and took the glass she handed him. 'Thanks,' he said as he sat down. 'This is just what I need.'

Thea had hoped that it would be easier in the dark, sitting where they always sat, but there was an edginess to the atmosphere that had never been there before. She longed to tell him how much she loved him, but she didn't know how. It wasn't the kind of thing you could just blurt out in the middle of the conversation, was it? *Oh, by the way, I'm in love with you.*

So she sat and twisted her fingers in her lap and tried to get back that wonderful sense of certainty she had had in Agios Nikolaos.

'You're very quiet tonight,' said Rhys after a while. 'What are you thinking about?'

About loving you. About wanting you. About needing you. About how I'm going to manage without you.

She didn't say any of those things, of course. She looked down into the glass she was turning slowly between her fingers. 'Oh…about tomorrow being our last night. I can't believe it's over.'

There, another opening for him. *It doesn't have to be over.* How easy would it be for him to say that?

'No, the last two weeks have gone quickly, haven't they?'

He looked up from his drink with a ghost of a smile. 'I've had a good time.'

Oh, dear, it was all beginning to sound very final. Thea swallowed.

'Me, too.'

She was just going to have to say something herself. If only she didn't feel so ridiculously shy. It was so *silly*, too. They were friends. She had never had any problem talking to him when she hadn't known that she was in love with him.

The silence began to twang.

OK, Thea told herself. Take it easy. Begin by saying that there's something you want to say to him, and take it from there.

Shoulders back. One deep breath. Two.

She had just opened her mouth when Rhys put down his glass with a click and stood up.

'I should go.' He sounded terse and so unlike himself that Thea, already thrown off by being interrupted just when she had plucked up the courage to tell him how she felt, could only gape at him.

'What's the matter?'

He couldn't go yet. Not now, just when she was ready to tell him the truth.

'Nothing...well, *something*, I suppose.' For the first time he seemed unsure of himself. 'But it's nothing to do with you,' he assured her. 'That is, it *is* about you, but—'

Rhys broke off and swore, raking his hands through his hair in frustration.

Thea had never seen him like this before, and it helped her to pull herself together.

'Rhys, sit down,' she said.

He stared at her for a moment and then sat abruptly.

Thea shifted round in her chair so that she was facing him. 'Now, tell me.'

'I was thinking about what you said,' said Rhys after a long, long pause.

'Something *I* said? What about?'

'About making the most of what was left of the holiday.'

He looked squarely into her eyes, and it was as if all the air had been sucked out of Thea's lungs.

'And I thought about how much I wanted to kiss you today,' he went on, his voice very deep and very low. 'I know it's just a holiday thing, and you're still confused and hurt about Harry, but today in the sea, when I was holding you, I wanted to forget all that and kiss you anyway.'

'Why didn't you?' asked Thea, her mouth so dry that the words came out as barely more than a husky whisper.

Rhys sighed and leant forward to rest his arms on his knees, looking away from her. 'Because it would have been a mistake.'

'Would it?'

'We're going home tomorrow, Thea. You know what these things are like.'

'What things?' she asked unsteadily, but she knew what he was going to say already.

'Being on holiday. You get thrown together, the way we have been, and everything is much more intense than it is at home, but it's not real. This is a time out of time. Right now, with the stars and the smell of the garden and the warm breeze, this seems like the only reality there is, but when we get back to London and our separate lives we'll realise that that's what real life is, and all this will be like a dream.'

She hadn't wanted him to say it, but he was right, wasn't he?

'I know,' she said.

Rhys's head came up at the sadness in her voice. 'I'm

sorry, Thea, I shouldn't have said anything. I didn't want to spoil things, especially now. You've been so wonderful.'

He dropped his head back into his hands. 'It's not as if I don't know how you feel about Harry. You probably can't wait to get back to London to see him. I've been there myself. I know what it's like to keep on loving someone and needing them, even when they've hurt you.'

Was that a way of telling her that Kate was right, and that he'd never got over Lynda?

Thea opened her mouth to put him right about Harry, but she had hesitated too long while she thought about what he had said, and Rhys was carrying on.

'It's not even as if I want to get distracted by a relationship with anyone. I came back to be a better father to Sophie, and that's what I need to concentrate on when I get home. I haven't got time to think about anybody else right now. Sophie hasn't had enough of my attention as it is over the last few years.'

Right, so now she knew. Thea stared out at the velvety sky embedded with stars and felt her heart constrict.

No more doubt, no more confusion. Rhys had told it like it was. He had no room in his life for her once they got home. He might want her now, but not for ever. Not even next week.

Thank God she hadn't blurted out that she loved him. It was all she could think.

And really, *did* she love him? Or was it, like he said, just a holiday thing? She had wondered herself for long enough, after all.

She had thought she was in love with Harry, too, and look how different the two men were. Rhys had none of Harry's dash and glamour. There was no reason to fall in love with him other than the fact that he *wasn't* Harry, and maybe that was all it was. She had turned to him because he was there and because he was different, just as Harry had turned to her after his relationship with Isabelle fell apart.

It would be easy to accept that.

But Thea couldn't. Deep down, she knew that moment in Agios Nikolaos was the only reality that meant anything. She did love Rhys, she was certain of it in the very core of her being, and for someone normally so wavering and unconfident and easily swayed it was a comfort to have for once such an unshakeable belief in her own feelings. It *was* real. She just had to accept one thing.

Rhys didn't love her back.

Thea drew a deep breath. She couldn't change his mind, not now. But there might be a chance to see him again when they got home. He might miss her.

Perhaps it was a mistake to think too much about the future. He was here, next to her in the dark, and he had said that he wanted to kiss her. And she wanted to kiss him too. Why deny that for the sake of a bit of pride?

She didn't need to tell him how she really felt. She didn't need to think about the future, how life would be without him. For now, all she needed was to kiss him and hold him and feel his arms around her. Like Scarlett O'Hara, she would worry about the rest tomorrow.

'There's no need to be sorry,' she said slowly. 'I know what you mean about this being a time out of time. You're right, it's not about real, or for ever, but the truth is that I wanted you to kiss me today too.'

He jerked round at that and his eyes fixed on her face.

'What are you saying?'

'This is our last night. Let's not waste it. You want to kiss me, and I want to kiss you. We both understand that it doesn't mean anything, that it's not about for ever.'

'Then what is it?' asked Rhys slowly, without taking his eyes from her face.

'A celebration of the last two weeks?' she suggested, getting up and going over to his chair. 'Clearing the air? A moment that's just for now, just between the two of us.'

He took her by the hand and drew her gently down into his lap. Taking a lock of her hair, he rubbed it between his fingers. 'Are you sure, Thea?'

Instead of answering, she shifted so that she could lean down and touch her lips to the pulse under his ear, the way she had fantasised about doing all day, all week.

'I'm sure.' She sighed into his throat. Now that she was here, close to him, with his arms around her, she couldn't stop kissing him. 'I'm sure,' she murmured again, nibbling little kisses along his jaw. 'This is just for us, just for now.'

And then he was turning his head and their lips met at last and the love and the longing shattered inside Thea. She melted into him with a tiny sigh of release. At last, at last, they were kissing, kissing properly, kissing not because Kate was watching, but because they both wanted to.

She couldn't get close enough to him, couldn't feel enough of him. Her lips and her fingers drifted over his face, his hair, his skin, those lovely sleek muscles in his shoulders, and all the while Rhys's hands were moving hungrily over her, exploring her, sliding under her skirt, smoothing over her thigh, until Thea thought she would dissolve with pleasure.

She clung to him, loving him, loving the feel of him, and their kisses grew deeper and more desperate. It was the first time that they had kissed like this, and the last time. However much Thea tried to shut the thought out, she couldn't.

This was the last time she would kiss Rhys. She couldn't bear it to end, couldn't bear time to have moved on to a time when it was over and all she had was the memory instead of this surge of sensation, this feeling of coming home, this sense that her life had been all about getting to this place and this time and this man.

But it did end, of course. Rhys's hand was tugging down the zip of her dress, his mouth burning along her clavicle when he forced himself to pause.

'The girls…'

Girls? What girls? Thea pressed closer and he drew a ragged breath.

'We need to stop while I still can.'

No, thought Thea. We need to *not* stop. We need to go up to the big white bed upstairs. We need to kiss each other all over. We need to never let each other go. But stop? No.

Girls… Rhys's voice reached her through a haze of desire, and a dullness crept over her as reality filtered back at last. Sophie and Clara were upstairs, probably still talking. Of course they had to stop. There would be no making love. It would be all letting go from now on.

Slowly she straightened. 'Of course, you're right,' she said, and from somewhere found a wavering smile for him. 'It was nice while it lasted, though!'

Something changed in his face. 'It was very nice,' he said softly.

She mustn't look at him. If she looked into his eyes she would blurt out the truth. Thea closed her eyes briefly to gather the strength to disentangle herself from him. Getting off his lap, she went over to the wall where the honeysuckle was entwined with jasmine and the heady scent enveloped her as she brushed against the flowers.

'And we've cleared the air,' she said, forcing brightness into her voice and keeping her back firmly turned to him. 'That's good.'

'I hope so.'

Thea heard the scrape of the chair as Rhys got to his feet and came to stand behind her. He put his hands on her shoulders and she squeezed her eyes shut against the temptation to lean back against him.

'You're a very special woman, Thea,' he said. 'I hope Harry's waiting for you at the airport.'

She didn't want Harry. She wanted Rhys, but how could she tell him that now? It doesn't mean anything, she had promised. It's not about for ever. It's about here and now. She couldn't change the rules now.

'It's our last day tomorrow,' he said, dropping his hands and stepping back. 'Let's make the most of that, too.'

They tried to make it a good day, but it just didn't work. Having chatted most of the night, Clara and Sophie were fractious and sulky about having to go home.

'I don't want to go,' grumbled Sophie.

'Your mum will be waiting to see you.' Thea tried to make her look on the bright side but it was hard when her own heart was like a leaden weight inside her. 'It'll be lovely to see her again, won't it?'

'Yes, but then I have to go back to school on Tuesday,' said Sophie glumly.

Well, she couldn't do anything about the start of term. Thea abandoned her efforts to be cheerful. Frankly, it was all she could do to keep the tears that clogged her own throat at bay.

If she had had the heart for it, she would have laughed at the idea of clearing the air with that kiss. Had they really believed that a kiss would somehow dissolve the tension between them?

Instead, it had had the opposite effect, so that now they could hardly talk to each other without the air thronging with memories of how it had felt to be able to kiss and to touch. Rhys made no reference to what they had shared, and neither did Thea, but she couldn't stop thinking about how right it had felt, about the sweetness and the gathering excitement. And with the good memories, like a bitter counterpoint, came the aching realisation that they wouldn't happen again. It was over.

None of them felt like going out. The children played in the pool and moaned about having to go back to school. Rhys was abstracted, and spent a lot of time checking the car.

Thea drifted drearily around the villa, picking up discarded towels and swimming costumes and books she had never got round to reading. Clara had spread her belongings all over the house. Thea found a Game Boy in the bathroom, a T-shirt on the floor in the living area, hair bands in the kitchen.

Nell would have made Clara pick them up herself, but Thea was glad of something to do other than ache for Rhys. It was her fault. She shouldn't have pushed that kiss. It hadn't made it better between them. It was much, much worse to know how close she had come and what she was going to miss.

It was almost a relief when it was time to have the promised drinks with the Paines. Instructed to be on their best behaviour, Sophie and Clara trailed over behind Rhys and Thea. 'We could be in the pool instead of having stupid drinks,' they grumbled.

'You can have a last swim later, but for now you can sit and be polite, or you won't be swimming again at all.' Rhys sounded sharp for him, and the girls exchanged glances.

As it turned out, Kate had no intention of the children taking part in the conversation anyway. She sent them inside to play cards with Hugo and Damian. 'I don't want you getting dirty,' she warned the boys.

Nick was despatched to find glasses, and she turned to Rhys and Thea. 'Now, we can sit and enjoy our last evening in peace! Hasn't it been a marvellous holiday?'

Thea thought about the sunlit days, about the smell of thyme and the sound of the cicadas. About sitting at local tavernas, and laughing with the girls, and the gleam of Rhys's smile in the darkness.

'It's been perfect,' she said, and glanced at him, sitting beside her with a set face. He didn't look as if he had had a perfect holiday. 'None of us want to go home,' she told Kate to distract her from the fact that Rhys clearly wasn't in a mood to make polite conversation.

'I always look forward to getting back,' said Kate briskly as Nick reappeared and to Thea's relief began handing out drinks. 'I like to have three weeks to recharge my batteries, but I'm itching to get to work now. There's always so much to sort out in the office. I sometimes wonder if it's worth going away at all.'

Right, what did three weeks with your children count for when it came to keeping your in-tray under control?

Thea's mind began to wander as Kate rabbited on about her job and how the entire legal system ground to a halt when she wasn't there to organise everybody. Rhys was staring morosely down into his glass, and she remembered how he had smiled the night before as he'd pulled her down into his lap, and her body clenched with longing.

'I see you haven't got a ring yet.' Thea was caught unawares when Kate switched the subject without warning and fixed an eagle eye on her naked hand. 'I'd have thought you would take the opportunity to get one while you're here. I mean, it's not that long until the wedding, is it?'

Thea moistened her lips. 'No, but there's no hurry. We thought we'd wait until we got home.'

'What have you got in mind? Diamonds, I suppose?' Kate

looked complacently at the massive cluster of diamonds on her own finger.

'Diamonds would be too cold for Thea.' Rhys's voice was curt as he took an unexpected part in the conversation. He took Thea's hand and studied it as if picturing a ring on her finger. 'She needs a different stone—a sapphire, perhaps?'

'I love sapphires,' stammered Thea, agonizingly aware of his touch.

'Oh.' Kate looked down her nose. 'Well, if that's what you like…Nick, go and see what those children are doing,' she snapped suddenly. 'They're making a lot of noise in there. I don't want Hugo and Damian running around.'

Poor Nick rose obediently, and she turned back to Rhys and Thea. 'I must confess I always think sapphires a little bit…' she searched for an alternative to common, which she was clearly longing to say '…ordinary,' she decided eventually. 'Diamonds are classic, so simple and elegant.'

'Well, I'm an ordinary person,' said Thea, trying to make a joke of it, but Rhys's brows drew together and he looked more forbidding than she had ever seen him.

'You're not ordinary,' he snapped. 'And nor are sapphires. They're beautiful and warm. Like Thea,' he finished, looking challengingly at Kate.

'The one advantage of going home is that we won't be exposed to that woman any longer,' said Rhys under his breath when they finally managed to leave. 'For the first two minutes you think she's not as bad as you remembered, and after five minutes you're ready to scream at how insufferable she can be. I don't know how Nick puts up with her.'

'I think he's worse,' said Thea. 'He spent half an hour showing me how his mobile phone works!'

They had gathered up Sophie and Clara, Clara in very

bad odour with Kate again for inciting the boys into playing hide-and-seek, first in the house and then in the garden, as a result of which all four of them were extremely grubby. Now they were sitting by the pool in the dark while the girls had their promised last swim, much to the envy of Hugo and Damian.

'You'll have a hard time shaking her off,' said Thea, desperate to keep the conversation going. She wasn't sure how to deal with Rhys in this new, grim mood. 'Did you hear her suggesting that we go over to their house for dinner one night so that we could compare photos?'

'I did. I also heard you say that would be lovely!'

'I had to say something,' she protested. 'I could hardly tell her we wouldn't be seeing each other, let alone them, could I?'

He glanced at her and then away. 'No,' he agreed in a flat voice.

'Kate's the kind of person who follows up invitations like that, too,' Thea warned. 'She'll track you down via Lynda and keep on and on at you until you agree to go, so you'd better be ready to explain why I'm not around.'

Rhys stared at the pool, which was unfamiliar in the darkness. 'I'll just say we've split up.'

'She'll ask you why. The Kates of this world always do.'

'I'll tell her that you snore,' he said with the first glimmer of humour he had shown all evening, and Thea was so relieved to see it that she even managed a laugh.

'You dare!'

'No, I'll tell her the truth,' said Rhys after a moment and she stared at him.

'What?'

'Oh, not about the pretending,' he said. 'I'll just explain that when I met you, you were on the rebound from a previous affair, but when you got home your old boyfriend was waiting for you and you realised that you'd made a mistake. I hope it'll be true, too—the bit about Harry waiting for you, anyway. You deserve the best.'

Why was he so keen on her getting back together with Harry, anyway? Thea wondered crossly. She was sick of hearing how much he hoped Harry would come up trumps. And she would decide who was best for her, thank you very much!

What was it with men, always telling you how you deserved someone better than them, as if you couldn't work out for yourself who you wanted? Nell said it was a way of avoiding responsibility.

'What "you deserve someone better than me" actually means is "I can't be bothered to make the effort for you",' she had told Thea.

So by pushing her towards Harry, Rhys could pretend that her falling in love was nothing to do with him, Thea thought, welcoming the way her resentment was growing. It was easier to feel angry than to bear the aching emptiness of imagining life without him.

He liked her, he'd wanted her last night, and he'd been in a bad mood all day at the thought of saying goodbye, but none of that was enough to make him stop and think that maybe he could change his mind, that he could be a good father and still have a relationship. That all he needed to do was tell her that he loved her and they could both be happy.

But it was easier to believe that Harry was responsible for making her happy, wasn't it? Rhys could reassure himself that it was nothing to do with him. He had kissed her and held her and listened to her and made her laugh and smiled at her, but hey, it wasn't his fault that she had fallen in love with him, was it?

And it wasn't really, Thea realised sadly. She had fallen in love with him all by herself.

'It'll be a relief not to have to pretend any more, anyway,' Rhys said after a while.

For him, maybe. She was going to have to carry on, pretending that last night's kiss didn't mean anything to her, pretending that she didn't love him, pretending that she was bright and cheerful and that her heart wasn't breaking even as she smiled.

'Yes. Still, it's been two weeks to remember. It's not every holiday you get to be engaged!'

Or fall in love.

'I'm sorry you won't be getting that sapphire ring.' At least now Rhys was making the effort to play along, to make these last few hours bearable.

Thea managed a brilliant smile. 'Ah well, better luck next time! You never know, maybe Harry will come through after all.'

Although Harry would opt for diamonds if he did. He would never think about buying her sapphires because they were warm and beautiful and reminded him of her.

Another silence fell.

'The girls are going to miss each other,' she said at last.

'They can meet up in London. They don't live that far away from each other, so I'm sure we can organise something.'

We presumably meant him and Lynda, though, or possibly him and Nell, Thea thought with a tinge of jealousy. Rhys would probably meet her sister, who had always been so much prettier, so much nicer, so much more sensible. Nell was exactly the kind of woman Rhys would fall for if he ever let himself.

Oh, she could probably arrange to be around sometimes, but what would be the point? Rhys had made it very clear that he didn't want a relationship, and Thea was sick of falling in love with men who didn't love her back.

That was one pattern she was going to break, she vowed. She was just going to have to bandage up her heart and get on with her life, and maybe one day she would meet a man who was prepared to love her wholeheartedly, the way she needed to be loved.

As long as she didn't spend her life wishing that man could be Rhys.

CHAPTER EIGHT

THEA stood in the baggage claim hall and watched the luggage juddering slowly around the carousel. It had been a long, dreary journey, starting in the small hours, and she was gritty-eyed with exhaustion and the sheer strain of keeping tears at bay for so long.

No sign of their cases yet, and they seemed to have been standing there for hours. Maybe they were lost. Thea couldn't decide whether that would be a good thing or not. It would delay the moment of saying goodbye for a few minutes longer, but she was dreading losing control so much that part of her longed to get it over with.

Rhys was stepping forward and lifting a suitcase off the carousel, and the next moment Clara was at her elbow, pointing. 'There's my case! And that's Sophie's, look.'

Let mine be lost, prayed Thea in panic, suddenly faced with the fact that as soon as her case appeared there would be no reason to stand here next to Rhys any longer. She would have to walk out into the arrivals hall and into her old life, and he would be gone.

But here it came, wedged between a set of golf clubs and a battered rucksack. For a moment, Thea was tempted to pretend that she hadn't seen it, but Clara was already pointing it out to Rhys, who lifted it easily off the carousel and put in on their trolley.

'Ah, there you are!' Kate came bustling up. 'We're all ready to go, so we'll say goodbye. It's been super to meet you.'

She thrust her cheek forward for an air kiss, and Thea

dutifully obliged. 'I presume I can reach you at Rhys's number? I'll give you a call,' she went on without waiting for Thea's reply, 'and we'll fix up supper. Now, must dash. Hugo, Damian! Come along!'

She breezed off, utterly sure of herself and everybody else, and Thea and Rhys were left alone, isolated in the middle of the crowded hall.

'How are you getting home?' asked Rhys stiltedly. 'I left the car here, so we could give you and Clara a lift if you wanted.'

Thea could have wept. 'Nell's going to meet us. She's not up to driving, but I'm sure my father will have brought her in the car.'

Why did she have to have a close and loving family? Right then, Thea would willingly have disposed of them all if she could only have a little longer with Rhys.

'I see,' he said. 'Good. Well, I'm glad you won't be struggling with those cases on the tube.'

'No, we'll be fine.'

How had it come to this? It wasn't that long since she had been lost in his arms, and now they were reduced to small talk.

'So,' said Rhys after a moment. 'It looks like this is it.'

The breath leaked out of Thea's body. 'Yes.'

With every fibre of her being she longed for him to suggest meeting up some time, ask for her number, anything to give her hope that he was thinking about seeing her again, but he was giving Clara a goodbye hug and making her giggle, so it looked as if that was that.

Thea kissed Sophie. 'I'll miss you,' she told her.

'When will I see you again?' asked Sophie, clinging to her.

'I'm…not sure, Sophie. Some time, I hope.'

'Soon?'

'I hope so.' What else could she say?

Sophie let her go reluctantly and turned to hug Clara, and the moment Thea had been dreading had come.

She made herself smile at Rhys. The smile came out a bit wavery, but it was the best she could do, and at least she wasn't throwing herself on his chest, wailing and screaming and begging him not to let her go, which was what she felt like doing. She hoped he was grateful.

'Well...' she said and kept the smile fixed in place with an enormous effort.

'Thea—' said Rhys, and then stopped.

Her heart was hammering painfully. 'Yes?' she prompted when he didn't go on, but he had clearly changed his mind about whatever it was he had been going to say.

'Just...thanks for everything.'

'I should be thanking you,' she managed.

'What for?'

'For looking after us and driving us around,' she said. 'We'd never have left the pool if it hadn't been for you.'

And she would never have had that wonderful moment of knowing that she had found him and that he was all that she would ever want.

Reaching up, she kissed him, just on the cheek, but her lips touched the corner of his mouth. She felt his hands close hard around her for a moment, holding her still, and then he released her, letting her step back.

'Goodbye.' Her voice cracked slightly and she drew a steadying breath as she took hold of the baggage trolley. She couldn't let go now. 'Come on,' she said to Clara. 'Let's see if we can find Mum.'

She made herself walk away from Rhys without looking back. It was one of the hardest things she had ever done. Hardly aware of where she was going, she pushed the trolley through Customs, and suddenly they were out into the

Arrivals Hall, disorientated for a moment by finding themselves faced with an enormous crowd of people waiting to greet friends and family.

They hesitated, scanning the faces. 'There she is!' cried Clara as she spotted the familiar figure at last, and she rushed over to her mother, almost knocking her off her crutches. 'Mum! Mum, we had such a cool time!'

Thea followed more slowly and was greeted by a warm hug from her father who, as expected, had driven the car for the still-incapacitated Nell. 'Hello, love. You don't look too happy for someone who's just had two weeks in Crete.'

'I'm fine.' She hugged her father back, feeling awful because over his shoulder she was trying to catch a last glimpse of Rhys. It was no good, anyway. He had already gone.

'I'm just tired,' she told him as he let her go. 'We had a very early start.'

'Well, I've got some news that might make you feel better,' said Nell, kissing her sister.

Right then, the only thing that could make Thea feel better was to see Rhys pushing his way through the crowds towards her, but she managed a smile for Nell.

'Oh?'

'Harry rang.'

Harry. How odd. He had been the beat of her heart for over a year, and when she had left for Crete she would have given everything she possessed to know that he would contact her sister.

And now…now she couldn't remember why it had mattered so much.

'Really?' she said, wanting to sound thrilled for Nell's sake, but obviously not being convincing enough. Nell looked puzzled, as well she might, having put up with months of Thea obsessing about Harry.

'Poor Thea, you *are* tired, aren't you?'

'What did Harry say?'

'That he had been trying to phone you but couldn't get a reply, and that he was worried about you. I did point out that he had had two months to ring you and he hadn't, so it was a bit much to start worrying about you now. In the end, I told him that you were fine and on holiday, so if he wanted to talk to you he was just going to have to wait. I didn't think it would do him any harm after all the waiting around he's made *you* do.'

'Quite,' agreed Thea with a twisted smile. Harry must have been worried if he had rung Nell. The two of them had never got on, and he wouldn't have appreciated getting the sharp end of a devoted sister's tongue.

'You know I've never had much time for Harry,' said Nell, 'but he did sound suitably apologetic, and so desperate to get hold of you that I guess that he's got something to say that you'll want to hear. I told him that you would be back today, so he'll probably ring you later.

'I hope that's OK,' she finished, looking understandably anxious at Thea's lack of enthusiasm. By rights, Thea should have been dancing around the airport shouting and singing with relief.

'Of course.' Thea smiled widely until her jaw ached to show just how happy she was. 'Thanks, Nell. I just hope he doesn't ring until I've had a chance to catch up on my sleep.'

If only sleep was all she needed. Thea went to bed that night hoping that she would wake up and realise that she had just been confused, and that away from the bright light and hot hillsides of Crete Rhys would seem as distant and unreal as Harry had done when she was there.

Only it didn't work like that. In a last burst of summer, just in time for the start of school, London was hot and sunny, but for once the glorious weather wasn't enough to lift Thea's spirits.

She woke the next morning with a leaden sense of despair. Post-holiday blues, she told herself firmly. It was Monday and she had to go back to work, sunshine or no sunshine. No wonder she was depressed.

But that didn't account for the rawness of her heart or the aching sense that a vital part of her was missing. Thea talked and smiled, and agreed with everyone at work that, yes, the weather in Crete had been great and that she had had a wonderful holiday, but inside she felt completely numb.

She tried telling herself that she would get over Rhys the same way she had got over Harry, but it was different this time. When Harry had decided to leave she had felt miserable and hurt and disappointed at the way things had worked out, but there had always been that glimmer of hope too to console her.

She hadn't felt desolate without Harry, the way she was desolate without Rhys. She hadn't had this terrible sense that life without him was empty and meaningless, the way it was empty and meaningless now, and the thought of the future, stretching inutterably bleak and lonely before her, hadn't been unendurable, the way it was unendurable now.

By the end of the week Thea was exhausted by the simple effort of getting from day to day, and she was beginning to feel desperate. She couldn't go on like this. Surely she would start to feel better soon.

Dutifully, she took her photos in to be developed, but when she went to pick them up she realised that she couldn't bear to look at them, so she sent them to Clara instead.

'They're wonderful,' Nell said when she rang up to thank her. 'It looks so beautiful, and it was great to see Sophie and Rhys after hearing so much about them from Clara.'

Rhys. Just the sound of his name was enough to make Thea flinch with longing.

'Why don't you come over for supper?' Nell went on. 'There's so much to talk about!'

The two sisters had always been close and it didn't take Nell long to realise that there was more amiss with Thea than the shock of going back to work when she saw her.

'Is it that bloody Harry again?' she demanded fiercely. 'Didn't he ring after all that?'

'Yes, he rang,' said Thea, remembering how odd it had been to hear Harry's voice again.

'What did he have to say for himself?'

Thea let out a long breath. 'He wanted to try again. He said that he loved me.' Once, less than a month ago, his call would have been a dream come true, but when Harry had rung she had found herself doodling as she listened to him.

'He said that he had had plenty of time to think over the summer and that he realised that he had had trouble cutting himself off from Isabelle when their relationship ended.'

'Well, that's one way of describing being kept dangling on the end of a string, I suppose,' said Nell sarcastically.

'According to Harry, Isabelle has found someone new to lean on, so everything would be different for us now.'

Nell sniffed, profoundly unimpressed. 'I suppose you realise that as soon as her new guy takes off she'll be snapping her fingers for Harry again?'

'Yes, I know,' said Thea with a tired smile, and Nell put down her glass and looked at her sharply.

'So what did you say?'

'I said that I thought it was too late and that I wasn't going to settle for being second best any more.'

What she hadn't told him, but what she had thought, was that meeting Rhys had made her realise that she wanted to be loved and needed for herself, that she wanted to be essential to the man she loved, not just a diversion or a fall-back position.

Nell sat back, looking relieved. 'Good for you!'

'Aren't you going to say "I told you so"?' asked Thea wryly.

'That's the last thing you want to hear when things go wrong,' said Nell, 'and I should know! People said it to me often enough when Simon left,' she added with a touch of bitterness.

'But I can't pretend I don't think you made the right decision telling Harry where to get off,' she went on. 'I couldn't see that he was ever going to make you happy.'

'No, I know that now.'

Nell looked concerned at the flatness in Thea's voice. 'Are you OK? Not regretting it?'

'No.' Thea shook her head. 'I'm fine. I'm just...tired, I suppose.'

'You can't still be tired! You've been back a week—' Nell broke off, her face clearing. 'It's Rhys, isn't it?'

'I don't know what you mean,' said Thea feebly, but her face must have given the game away.

'Come on, Thea.' Her sister shook her head at her own obtuseness. 'I should have clicked before, but I thought you were still wrapped up in Harry. Clara's done nothing but talk about Sophie and Rhys all week. She told me all about your engagement.'

'It wasn't an engagement,' Thea protested. 'We were pretending, as Clara knows perfectly well.'

'Pretending to be in love is a dangerous game,' said Nell. 'It's got a nasty habit of turning into the real thing without you noticing!'

'Why didn't you warn me about that before I went to Crete?' said Thea miserably.

'Well, I thought you'd be too busy looking after my

daughter to get involved in mock engagements with strange men,' teased Nell, but Thea couldn't even muster a smile. 'Look, what's the problem, anyway? He looks really nice in the photos and Clara likes him a lot. She thinks he's perfect for you.'

'I think he's perfect for me too. It just doesn't work the other way round. I'm not perfect for Rhys.' To her horror, Thea heard her voice crack on his name, and she put a hand up to cover her trembling mouth.

There was nothing she could do about the hot tears scalding her eyes, though, and Nell pushed back her chair quickly and came round to give her sister a comforting hug.

'Hey! Come on, it can't be that bad!'

'It is,' wept Thea, losing her battle against tears. 'What's wrong with me, Nell?'

'Nothing's wrong with you!'

'Then why do I keep falling in love with men who can't love me back?'

'How do you know Rhys doesn't love you?' asked Nell, handing over a box of tissues.

Thea took one and blew her nose noisily. 'He doesn't want to get involved. He told me he didn't have the time or energy for a proper relationship.'

'Hmm.' Nell looked sceptical. 'Spending two weeks with you and doing everything together doesn't strike me as the right way to go about not getting involved!'

'It was just a holiday thing, and anyway nothing happened, not really. We were just friends, and now... Oh, God, I miss him so much, Nell!' Thea dissolved into fresh tears and her sister patted her back absently, her expression slightly puzzled.

'Give him a ring if you miss him.'

'I can't!'

'Why not? You just said you were friends. Friends are allowed to ring each other.'

'It's not like that,' said Thea indistinctly through another tissue. 'Rhys made it clear that his priority is to spend time with Sophie. He would feel guilty getting emotionally involved with anyone else when the whole point of him coming home was to be with his daughter and try and make up for the time he's lost. He thinks he needs to concentrate on her for the time being, and I can't argue against that, can I?'

Nell wasn't looking convinced. 'It's all very well in theory, but I can't see that devoting his entire life to his daughter is particularly healthy in practice. And once you've got used to having someone to be with, even if you are just pretending, you're going to miss them when they're not there any more. Anyway, from what Clara told me, I wouldn't be at all surprised if he got in touch with you.'

'He doesn't have my number.' Thea scrubbed at her face with a tissue. 'He didn't even ask for it.'

'He looked pretty competent to me,' Nell pointed out. 'I don't think finding out your number would be much of a challenge for him.'

'If he'd missed me, he would have called by now,' said Thea with one of those ragged sighs that came after crying. There was no use in getting her hopes up. 'He won't ring.'

That was Friday evening, and on Saturday Thea let herself into her flat and dumped a load of carrier bags on the kitchen floor. She had spent most of the morning fighting her way around the supermarket and had suddenly understood why everybody else hated it so much.

Thea had always secretly enjoyed pushing her trolley up and down the aisles, tossing in whatever happened to catch her eye, but today she had been completely lacking in inspiration. Even the cheese counter had failed to cheer her up.

Typical! All those years longing for her appetite to desert her, and now she was too miserable to enjoy the fact that for once in her life comfort eating had lost its appeal.

Her fridge had never looked so spartan. Thea finished unpacking the last of the bags and decided to go wild and celebrate with a glass of mineral water. Perhaps this was the start of a new, healthier her, and she would look back in years to come at this miserable weekend as a turning point in her life? She might screw up her face in an effort to remember why she had been so unhappy and why Rhys had mattered so much.

There, now she was beginning to think more positively, Thea congratulated herself. She was letting herself imagine a time when none of this would matter. That had to be a step in the right direction. She was well on the way to recovery.

The light on her answer machine was flashing, and she pushed the play button idly as she found a glass and unscrewed the top of the water.

'Thea, it's Rhys. I got your number via Sophie and—'

Thea jerked involuntarily at the sound of his voice, spilling water everywhere, and she leapt for the machine to save the message and play it again.

'...I got your number via Sophie and Clara, and eventually your sister, who sounds very nice. I wanted to ask you a favour, and wondered if you could give me a ring when you get in?'

He had left his number and signed off with a simple, 'Hope to talk to you soon.'

Thea listened to the message three times, her hand shaking so much that she couldn't write down his number properly. The figures staggered over the page as if some drunken spider was in charge of her pen, and all the time her heart sang, It was him, it was him! He called me!

Her knees felt quite weak by the time she had finished, and she had to sit down, staring down at the piece of paper clutched in her hand.

So much for being well on the way to recovery! The sound of his voice was all it had taken to put her right back at square one.

Unable to help herself, Thea reached out and played the message once more. It wasn't exactly lover-like and he hadn't said anything about missing her, it was true. But he had thought about her, he had called her! Thea's spirits, their downward spiral abruptly halted, were now zooming skywards once more.

What was this favour he wanted to ask? Once more her finger pressed the play button, convinced that she might have missed something vital the first ten times she had listened to it. But no, it was infuriatingly uninformative. He had a favour to ask, and he wanted her to ring him.

If she wanted to find out what it was, the obvious thing would be to ring him, wouldn't it?

She rang Nell instead.

'Didn't I say he'd ring?' her sister greeted her. 'He sounds absolutely lovely, I must say. We had quite a chat.'

'Nell, if you said anything about me…'

'Of course I didn't,' Nell soothed her. 'I just said that I'd heard a lot about him from Clara. I did say that I was sure you'd be pleased to hear from him, though. Now, why are you ringing me and not him?'

'I'm just so nervous,' confessed Thea. 'I'm terrified I'll say something stupid and make a mess of it.'

'What's there to make a mess of? He asked you to ring him. Call him back, listen to what he wants and if this mysterious favour is a reasonable one—and it probably is, as

Rhys sounds a reasonable man—all you have to do is to say OK. And then you'll get to see him again, which is what you want. If he wants you to do something unreasonable, you just have to say no. You might not get to see him in that case, but if he's being that unreasonable you probably won't want to, will you?'

Right. Funny how easy it was to think clearly when it wasn't your heart that was hammering in your throat, or your stomach churning with nerves. Thea stared at the phone when Nell had rung off and concentrated on breathing calmly. Several times she reached out to pick it up once more, only to snatch her hand back at the last minute as her nerve failed her.

OK. More deep breaths. In, out. In, out. Pick up phone. Dial number.

Thea listened to Rhys's phone ring. Once, twice, three times. He was out. Was she going to have to go through this all over again, or could she cope with leaving a message? Oh, God…

'Rhys Kingsford.'

Her hands were so slippery by this stage that she almost dropped the phone when he answered.

'It's me,' she said stupidly. Not that he would recognize who 'me' was with her voice wavering up and down like a demented duck. 'Thea.'

'Thea!'

She could almost hear him smile, and he sounded so warm and so strong and so familiar that the terrible jitters began to subside somewhat.

'It's good to hear from you,' he was saying. 'Thank you so much for ringing back. How are you?'

'Oh…fine, fine,' she lied. 'How about you?'

They exchanged rather stilted chit-chat for a bit. Thea asked about Sophie, and going back to work, and whether he'd had his photos developed, while what she really wanted to ask was whether he'd missed her, if he remembered kissing her, if he thought he could ever bring himself to love her.

'You mentioned a favour,' she said at last, desperate in case she ended up blurting one of them out anyway.

'Yes,' said Rhys slowly. 'I feel a bit awkward about it, to tell you the truth. I'd rather explain face to face, if possible. Look, I don't suppose you're free any time this weekend?

Not the time to start playing hard to get, thought Thea. 'When were you thinking of?'

'Any chance of this evening?'

It was nice of him to sound dubious. Any self-respecting girl would be out partying of a Saturday evening, but Thea had long abandoned her pride as a lost cause.

'Fine by me,' she said.

They agreed to meet at a wine bar Thea knew, about halfway between them. 'See you there at seven, then,' said Rhys as he rang off.

That only left Thea six hours to dither around and let the jitters build up all over again.

It was no use pretending that he had sounded remotely lover-like. He hadn't said anything about missing her, so whatever Rhys had in mind it clearly *wasn't* a proposal of marriage or a suggestion that he might whisk her back to his house and ravish her.

Shame.

Still, she would see him; that was what mattered. Thea's senses sang at the prospect. She kept picking things up and putting them down again, forgetting what she had meant to do with them, unable to settle to anything.

Then there was deciding what to wear. That took *ages*. Naturally, she didn't want to look as if she was trying too hard, but on the other hand, what if the whisking and ravishing scenario materialised after all? She needed to make a bit of effort.

Reluctantly, Thea laid aside a flirty little skirt and opted for black trousers instead. At least they were well cut, and one advantage of the last miserable week was the fact that they fitted quite comfortably now. She would wear them with a pale pink cardigan that she had picked up for a song in the sales. It hit just the right note between classy and sexy, and had that irresistible softness that practically screamed *touch me*.

She saw Rhys as soon as she walked in the door that evening. He was sitting at a table, looking brown and self-contained, and somehow more definite than everybody else in the bar. Thea's jangling nerves stilled abruptly at the sight of him, and she filled instead with that wonderful sense of certainty she had felt in Agios Nikolaos. He was the man she loved and he was waiting there for her. For now that was all that she wanted.

Rhys got to his feet as he spotted her, and his expression made her feel ten feet tall. She smiled.

'Hello.'

'Thea, you look…wonderful!'

They faced each other, suddenly uncertain of the most appropriate way to greet each other and, after a moment, Thea leant forward and kissed him on the cheek.

'It's good to see you again, Rhys.'

A masterly understatement, if ever she made one. Her eyes devoured him, hardly able to believe that he was there and solid. She longed to be able to burrow into him, to sink on to his lap and kiss the way they had kissed in Crete, but Rhys was already heading to the bar to get her a drink, and she had to sit down instead and get her hands firmly under control.

She was very glad when he brought back a glass of wine. It gave her something to hold on to, and stopped her hands from wandering towards him of their own accord.

'I've been thinking about you a lot,' said Rhys, sitting next to her, tantalisingly close, but not close enough to touch.

Thea's heart lurched. Maybe she had it all wrong? Maybe he was thinking along ravishing lines after all?

'Oh?' she said unsteadily.

'I wondered if you'd heard from Harry since you got back.'

'Oh,' she said again, in a very different voice. 'Yes, yes, I did actually, but…' She trailed off. How could she explain to Rhys about Harry? He would never believe that she could have changed her mind so quickly and so completely.

He was waiting for her to finish, a look of concern on his face. 'It didn't work out,' was all she said in the end.

'I'm sorry.' He sounded as if he meant it.

'Honestly, I'm fine about it,' said Thea, summoning a bright smile to prove her point. 'Nell keeps telling me that it's all for the best, and I think she's right.'

She wondered about reassuring Rhys that she was heart whole and fancy-free, but decided that it was too much of a heavy hint. Surely he would have got the point that Harry was out of the picture, in any case, which left it wide open for any move he might want to make.

'Tell me about you, anyway,' she said when Rhys gave no sign of following up the opening she had offered. 'What's this favour you mentioned? Don't tell me you haven't been able to fob Kate off on the dinner party front?'

Rhys gave a twisted smile. 'This time it's not really Kate that's the problem,' he said. 'It's Sophie.'

'Sophie?' Thea echoed incredulously. 'What's wrong with her?'

'There's nothing wrong, she's fine,' he said hastily. 'She's just…well, prolonging our engagement, I guess you could say.'

'Prolonging…?' She stared at him. 'What do you mean?'

Rhys took his glass of beer and moved it around the table, as if making a pattern with the wet ring it left.

'It's all my fault, really,' he said. 'As expected, Kate told Lynda all about you but, instead of asking me about it, Lynda questioned Sophie. I should have realised she'd do that,' he added with a sigh.

'What did Sophie say?'

'She said it was all true, and that she really liked you. She certainly gave Lynda to understand that we were very serious. She told her that I was going to buy you a ring and that we were planning to get married at Christmas. They must have picked up more of our conversations than we realised.'

Thea grimaced slightly. 'How did Lynda react?'

'She was straight on the phone to me, demanding to know what was going on. I'd planned to tell her that there wasn't anything serious between us, and that if she asked I'd just say we'd decided to call it a day, but… Well, the truth is that I didn't want her to be able to accuse Sophie of not being completely honest. I should never have put her in that position to begin with.'

'So you played along?'

He nodded. 'At first I thought it would just be for another couple of weeks and then we'd go back to the original plan.'

Thea looked at him. 'It sounds like there's a "but" coming?'

'There is,' said Rhys. 'Now Lynda wants to meet you.'

CHAPTER NINE

SHE'S been quite insistent about it,' Rhys went on ruefully, 'and I'm running out of excuses. That's when I wondered if you would consider coming along and having a drink with Lynda, and pretending that you really are engaged to me for one more night.'

'So that's the favour?'

'That's the favour,' he said. 'I don't like to ask you, especially when you must still be upset about Harry, but it really would just be for one evening. It doesn't need to be a whole evening either. Just an hour or so would do.'

An hour or so. Was that all she was going to have with him? Thea's heart contracted. He seemed very keen to keep it short. But then, she didn't want to spend an entire evening with his ex-wife either, did she?

'Perhaps we could have dinner afterwards,' Rhys went on, and her spirits did an abrupt U-turn in 'mid nosedive. She could practically hear the squeal of slamming brakes and then the revving as they roared upwards once more.

OK, so it wasn't a passionate declaration of love, but at least they would be alone together. That had to be a step in the right direction.

'That would be lovely,' she said.

His face lit up. 'You mean you'll do it?'

'Of course,' said Thea. 'It's a bit late for me to object to pretending on principle, don't you think? Anyway, I'd like to see Sophie again. It'll be like old times. I've missed them,' she added lightly, wanting to say, I've missed you, but not quite daring, not yet.

Rhys looked at her, as if remembering how she had been in Crete, bare feet resting on the terrace wall, tousled hair tumbling to her shoulders, her skin luminous in the starlight.

'So have I,' he said.

The meeting with Lynda was eventually arranged for that Wednesday. Rhys and Thea agreed to meet at South Kensington station and catch the tube out to Wimbledon together after work.

This allowed Thea to spend Monday and Tuesday agonizing over the eternal question of what to wear. Kate would have told Lynda how hopelessly scruffy she had been in Crete, so she was determined to make an effort to look smart for once. It was going to be intimidating enough meeting the beautiful, successful, talented Lynda as it was without feeling her usual mess as well.

How come she had never possessed one of those outfits that were supposed to go effortlessly from day to evening? Thea chewed her thumb as she contemplated her wardrobe, depressed by the utter lack of anything remotely stylish that she could wear to the office, to have a drink with Lynda and then move on to dinner with Rhys. It was a pity he had already seen that pink cardigan.

In the end, she threw money at the problem and bought a little grey suit in her lunch hour on Tuesday. She had never owned anything classic before, and she was quite pleased with the effect, although she nearly lost her nerve when presented with the total. Still, it would have been silly not to take the ivory silk top that went so perfectly with it at the same time, and the shoes made sense too. Didn't they say you should always buy a complete outfit?

Thea scribbled her name and decided to worry about paying for it later. What was the point of having a credit card if you couldn't use it in an emergency like this?

Anyway, it was worth it, she thought, admiring herself in

the mirror on Wednesday morning. She should have tried the classy look before. It was just a shame she didn't have that lovely glossy blonde hair you could sweep up into a chignon. A mop of brown curls didn't have quite the same effect.

The downside was putting up with everyone in the office gawping at her as if she had never worn a skirt before. She got a bit sick of people telling her how smart she looked and then asking what was up, and her boss claimed to have hardly recognized her, which was a bit much given that she was sitting at her usual desk and he could only see her top half anyway.

She realised what he meant, though, when she saw Rhys that evening. She hardly recognized him, either. It was raining and she was sheltering inside the entrance, shaking out her umbrella, when she saw him running across the road. He was wearing a dark grey suit and tie, which surprisingly suited his austere features, but made him look very different from the lean, brown, outdoors man she remembered from Crete.

Conscious of a quite ridiculous feeling of shyness, Thea waved as he reached the ticket barriers and looked around for her.

'I'm here,' she said. 'You ran right past me!'

'I didn't recognize you,' said Rhys, just as her boss had. He looked her up and down, taking in the suit and the elegant new shoes, and mentally comparing her to the woman he had known in Crete, with her bright, creased sundresses and casual tops. 'I've never seen you in a suit before. You look…quite different.'

'Do you know, I was going to say *exactly* the same thing to you,' Thea confided, and felt that moment of shyness evaporate as he managed to grin and grimace at the same time.

'I hate wearing a tie,' he said, running a finger around his collar. 'I never needed one out in the desert. I forgot that coming back to London would mean putting on a suit every day.'

Thea eyed the constant stream of people heading purposefully into the station, determined to get home out of the rain as soon as they could. 'I don't suppose you did a lot of commuting in the Sahara either.'

'No.' Rhys sighed a little. 'I can't say that I enjoy it, but then who does?'

And it meant that he could see Sophie. If it hadn't been for her, he would be out under the vast desert sky, in the heat and the space and the light. He belonged out there, not here in a suit and tie, with crowds pushing past them to get through the ticket barriers, puddles on the floor and the dank smell of wet coats.

For the first time Thea realised what he had given up to do the right thing by his daughter. She wished she could find a way to tell him that she admired him without sounding patronising, but in the end all she could think of to do was to lay a hand on his arm.

'Sophie's worth it, though, isn't she?'

Rhys looked down into Thea's warm grey gaze. 'Yes, she is,' he said, covering her hand with his own and tightening his clasp.

The suit might be different, but those light greeny-grey eyes were still the same, and they had the same transfixing effect on Thea, who felt herself melting inside, just the way she had in Crete. For a moment the two of them might have been back there, isolated in a private bubble from the rush hour crowds jostling around them.

It was Rhys who was jolted back to reality by a bump from a passing commuter. 'Oh, I nearly forgot,' he said as he slipped his hand inside his jacket and pulled out a little box. 'I bought you a ring to wear this evening.'

'That's not necessary, surely?' she said awkwardly.

He shrugged. 'I thought I might as well get something. It's the kind of detail that Lynda notices. Here, see what you think.'

Thea had little choice but to take the box from him. Opening it slowly, she saw the simple ring inside and her throat tightened.

'Sapphires,' she said, managing an unsteady smile.

'Did you think I'd forget?'

She glanced at him, knowing that they were both remembering that conversation on Kate's terrace. 'It seems a long time ago, doesn't it?' she said a little sadly.

There was a tiny pause.

'What do you think of it?' asked Rhys, nodding at the ring.

What did it matter what she thought of it? Thea wondered. It was only for this evening. She looked down at the box where the sapphires gleamed against a plain gold band.

'It's beautiful,' she said, and meant it.

'Try it on,' he said, taking the ring out of the box and sliding it on to her finger. 'I hope it fits. I had to guess at the size.'

It was a little loose, but not too bad. Thea bit her lip. It was impossible not to think of what it would feel like if this were for real, if he had bought her the ring because he loved her and needed her and wanted to spend the rest of his life with her, and not just to provide an extra detail to convince his ex-wife.

'Rhys, I—' She stopped at the sudden realisation that they were being watched.

'Aah!' A plump woman nudged her companion as she

spotted the ring on Thea's finger, and they both stopped to stare openly.

Within a matter of seconds, it seemed, Thea and Rhys had attracted a curious crowd. Some were watching in the hope of a sentimental scene, some were evidently up for any diversion from the usual routine, while others were simply staring because everybody else was staring.

'Say yes, darlin',' shouted a wag from the crowd and there was a ripple of laughter.

It was such an absurd situation to find themselves in at a tube station in the middle of a wet rush hour that Thea couldn't help laughing.

Rhys's lips were twitching too. 'I think you'd better say yes,' he murmured, 'or we might never get out of here!'

'Oh, all right, then,' said Thea loud enough for everyone to hear, and there was such a cheer that she began to think there might be something to be said for public proposals after all.

'Go on, give her a kiss!' someone else suggested and others took it up. 'Yes, give her a kiss!'

Thea's eyes met Rhys's. 'You started it,' she said, *sotto voce.*

A smile hovered around his mouth. 'And it would be a shame to disappoint them, wouldn't it?' he said as he reached out and gathered her into his arms.

A barrage of whistles and clapping broke out, but Thea hardly heard it. She melted into his kiss, flooded with a dazzling sense of coming home. It was so wonderful to be close to him again, to be able to kiss him back and feel his arms around her. Her own arms slid of their own volition beneath his jacket and tightened around his back, holding him close so that she would never have to bear to let him go.

But she had to, of course. 'Come on, move it along here.'

A bad-tempered official managed to push his way through the crowd at last and tapped Rhys on the shoulder. 'Find somewhere else to get engaged, mate,' he said to a chorus of boos. 'You're blocking the entrance here.'

'Sorry.' Rhys let Thea go and acknowledged the cheery crowd that was reluctantly dispersing with a lifted hand and a wry smile. 'I think we'd better go,' he said to Thea.

Somehow she found her travel pass, got through the barrier and down the steps to the platform. She felt utterly boneless—it was a surprise to find that she could stand up at all on her own, let alone walk—and so woozy that she was practically reeling along the platform. She was very glad Rhys was there beside her, the one fixed point in a swirling, spinning world.

'Well, at least we provided them with some entertainment,' he said dryly as they found a space to wait for the train.

'It was quite funny, really,' Thea managed.

He glanced at her and then away. 'Very funny,' he agreed, but not as if he found it very humorous.

They had to wait for ages for the Wimbledon train and, when it did arrive, it was packed. Thea didn't mind. She got to stand pressed up against Rhys.

'Do you want to hold on to me?' he asked as the doors squeezed shut and everybody held their breath.

Well, *there* was a question. Thea wondered what he would say if she told him that she did, she wanted to hold on to him for ever.

Except she knew what he would say, didn't she? He might be very nice about it, but essentially he would say what he had said in Crete, that for now the only person he wanted to hold on to was his daughter.

So she just nodded and took the opportunity to lean against him while she could. He was holding on to the overhead rail with one hand, his body braced against the lurching of the train, which meant that she could put an arm around his waist and balance against him.

It was a disappointment when a whole lot of passengers got off at Earl's Court. They found seats side by side. Thea stared up at an advertisement for cheap flights on the internet and tried not to think about reaching out for his hand, climbing into his lap, making him kiss her again…

The doors hissed open once more. They were only at Fulham Broadway. Thea sighed and fiddled with the unfamiliar ring on her finger. They couldn't sit in silence all the way to Wimbledon.

She cleared her throat. 'I presume we stick to the same story as before? About how we met and what I was doing pursuing you out to Crete?'

'I think that would be best, don't you?' said Rhys, who seemed annoyingly relaxed and not at all like someone who was longing to get her on her own so that he could kiss her properly in private.

'Is there anything I should know before I meet Lynda?'

'She can seem a little intimidating sometimes,' he said after thinking about it for a few moments, 'but that's just her manner. Don't let her put you off.'

If Rhys thought Lynda could be intimidating, Thea didn't give much for her own chances of not being put off by his ex. He had to be the least easily intimidated person she had ever met.

'I gathered from Kate that she's a very successful businesswoman.'

'She is. She's a clever woman, with a huge amount of drive and determination, and she's ambitious too. I remember when I asked her to marry me, I was amazed when she agreed. I never thought she'd settle for less than a millionaire.'

Oh, so he had been besotted enough to want Lynda, even thinking something like that about her. Thea's lips tightened at the thought of Rhys loving Lynda enough to risk rejection. How thrilled he must have been, how dazzled by her, when she agreed.

'You obviously didn't make the mistake of asking her in the middle of a tube station,' she said almost tartly, and Rhys was startled into a grin.

'No, I didn't do that.'

'How did you propose?' Thea asked in spite of herself.

'The usual clichés. A restaurant, candlelight, roses…I was very young,' he added, as if excusing himself.

'Oh, those old chestnuts,' said Thea enviously. She wouldn't have said no either if Rhys had laid on the clichés for her. 'I'm not sure I wouldn't prefer a wet tube station, myself,' she lied.

The corner of Rhys's mouth lifted as he looked at her, sitting bright-eyed in her suit, the raindrops still spangling the mass of brown hair. 'I'll remember that,' he said.

It was still raining when they eventually emerged from the underground station at Wimbledon, so they shared Thea's umbrella, walking close to keep as dry as possible. Thea normally hated the rain, but she would have been happy to have walked like that for hours with Rhys. All too soon, though, he was indicating a house ahead.

'Here we are.'

They stood in the shelter of the porch and Thea shook the worst of the rain from her umbrella.

'Nervous?' asked Rhys as they rang the doorbell.

'Should I be?'

'You'll be fine,' he reassured her.

The door opened, and Thea realised that (a) he hadn't answered her question directly, and (b) exactly why he had used that reassuring tone of voice.

She had been expecting someone crisp and conventional like Kate, but Lynda wasn't like that at all. Instead she was dark and dramatic, almost exotic-looking, with huge brown eyes and a cascade of beautiful dark hair down her back. Very slender—infuriatingly so, in fact—she wore black jeans that clung to her perfectly yoga-honed body and a sexy, sleeveless vest that Thea wouldn't have been able to carry off in a million years.

Just to make Thea feel even more lumpy and bourgeois, she was barefoot, presumably to show off her toe-ring. The message, clearly, was that Lynda was too intense and spiritual to waste her time with superficial things like shoes.

Thea was torn between intense irritation and wanting to sink through the floor. She had seen Lynda's eyes flick dismissively over the suit she had been so proud of. It had felt so smart and sexy that morning; now it seemed merely cheap and conservative and utterly, utterly boring. She would have been better off in her crumpled sundress.

Why hadn't Rhys warned her? Thea raged internally. It was a bit late to hint at the need to be nervous when she was actually at the door!

He was kissing Lynda's cheek, all very friendly and amicable. No bitter divorce for the likes of Lynda, obviously. 'I've brought Thea to meet you, as promised,' he said.

'Hello.'

Thea's smile felt stiff as she held out her hand. No doubt shaking hands was as bourgeois and outdated as wearing a suit to work. Lynda probably expected her to exchange some spiritually sound greeting, chink their crystals together, perhaps, or press their hands to heart and forehead.

Lynda didn't exactly shun her hand, but she clasped it warmly between both of hers as if to indicate that a simple shake would be too repressed and buttoned up for her.

'It's marvellous to meet you at last, Thea,' she said, her voice deep and breathy. 'Come in.'

She ushered them into an incredibly cool, uncluttered room that had Feng Shui all over it. Comparing it to her own unbelievably chaotic sitting room, with its mismatched curtains and junk shop furniture, Thea suppressed a sigh. Funny, just when you thought you could feel as inadequate as it was possible to feel, you could manage to feel it just that little bit more.

The sound of feet charging down the stairs made her turn, and the next second Sophie burst into the room. 'Thea!'

'Sophie!' Thea was so glad to see her and to find her exactly the same that tears pricked at her eyes as she hugged the little girl. 'I've missed you! So has Clara.'

'Oh, yes, I've heard a lot about Clara.' Lynda's laugh held a slight edge, and Thea guessed that she had been talking to Kate. 'She sounds quite a character!'

'Yes, she is,' Thea agreed.

'Come and see my room,' said Sophie, tugging at her hand.

'Sophie,' Lynda interrupted reproachfully. 'Aren't you going to say hello to your father?'

'Sorry, Dad.' She ran over to give him a hug. 'I was just excited to see Thea again.'

He grinned down at her and tweaked her nose. 'I know how you feel, Sophie!'

'Come on, then, Thea.'

Sophie headed for the door and Thea hesitated. She could see that Lynda was looking a little tight-lipped, but when she glanced at Rhys he nodded encouragingly.

She admired Sophie's room, which looked remarkably like Clara's, right down to the photo board. In pride of place, she was interested to see, was a picture of the four of them by the pool in Crete.

Thea remembered the day Nick had taken it for them. Rhys had been at one end and Thea at the other, with Sophie and Clara in between them. They were all laughing, squinting a little into the sun, and they looked so happy and relaxed that Thea's heart contracted.

'We had a good time in Crete, didn't we?' she said to Sophie, who heaved a sigh.

'I asked Dad if we could go again with you next year.'

'What did he say?'

'He said, "We'll see",' said Sophie, and Thea couldn't help laughing at her disgusted expression.

'I'm afraid that's the kind of thing parents say!' She looked at her watch. 'I'd better go down and talk to your mum,' she said. 'That's why I came, really.'

'OK.'

Sophie jumped off the bed and took her back down to where whatever words Lynda and Rhys might have had about their daughter had obviously been resolved. As Thea came down the stairs she could see them through the open doorway. They were sitting together on the sofa, talking. Lynda was leaning earnestly towards Rhys, her dark eyes fixed on his face, and Thea's eyes narrowed suspiciously. Lynda's body language said that she still had a more than proprietorial interest in him.

Fixing on a bright smile, she let Sophie lead the way into the room.

'There you are!' Lynda uncoiled herself from the sofa and got to her feet. 'Come and have that drink, Thea. Rhys, you know where everything is, don't you?'

'Of course,' he said and smiled at Thea as he stood up. 'What would you like, darling?'

For a terrible moment, Thea thought that he was speaking to Lynda. Then she remembered the ring on her finger and the part she was supposed to be playing.

'My usual, please,' she said innocently. Let him make of that what he would!

'Can I have a lemonade?' asked Sophie.

'You know I won't have lemonade in the house,' said Lynda in a sharp voice. 'Rhys, you don't give her lemonade, do you?'

'Occasionally,' he said from the kitchen.

'I wish you wouldn't. Those drinks are full of additives.'

'Oh, Mum…'

'That's enough, Sophie. You're not having anything. Anyway, you haven't done your violin practice yet. Dad will come up and listen to you while I'm talking to Thea.'

'I want to stay with Thea,' grumbled Sophie and Lynda's fine brows drew together.

'Answering back seems to be a little habit you've picked up on holiday, Sophie,' she said, which Thea was sure was a dig at Clara. It sounded exactly like something Kate would say, anyway. 'I don't like it. Now, off you go.'

Sophie scuffed off crossly and could be heard stomping upstairs as Rhys came back in with a glass of white wine for Thea and some murky-looking juice for Lynda, who had sunk gracefully into the lotus position on the floor.

'Organic cranberry and ginger,' she said, following Thea's appalled gaze, and took a sip. 'Delicious.'

'I'm sure,' said Thea politely, glad that Rhys had given her wine. She had a feeling she was going to need it, even if it wasn't the gin and tonic she had been craving. No doubt they had too many additives to be allowed in Lynda's house too.

'Darling, I told Sophie you'd go and listen to her violin practice,' said Lynda as Rhys made to sit down next to Thea.

Darling, eh? Thea's eyes narrowed slightly. It would be interesting to know whether Lynda called everyone darling, or if it had been a deliberate slip in response to the fact that he had called Thea darling so obviously.

'You can take your drink with you,' Lynda was overriding Rhys's attempts to object. 'You're always saying you want to be more involved with what Sophie's doing,' she added reproachfully. 'Or is that just for effect?'

In the end, Rhys had little choice but to follow his daughter. He could hardly insist on staying when Lynda was so insistent and, anyway, Thea could see that the merest suggestion that he might not be prepared to pull his weight with Sophie had stung.

'Now,' said Lynda, turning back to Thea, 'we can have a good chat without him cramping our style.'

'Right,' said Thea a little nervously.

'I hope you won't think I'm nosy, but naturally I want to know as much as I can about anyone proposing to spend what will inevitably be a lot of time with my daughter.'

Well, that seemed fair enough. 'I can understand that.'

'And, then again, I'm still very fond of Rhys,' Lynda went on. 'If he really *has* found someone he can be happy with, no one would be more delighted than me, I promise you.'

She sighed and ran a hand through the dark rippling hair. 'I've felt so responsible for the fact that he's had such difficulty forming relationships since our divorce. I know I damaged him, and I want so much for him to recover, but...'

Ah. Thea had had a feeling that a but was coming.

Lynda lowered sweeping lashes. 'I don't quite know how to say this,' she said, her voice positively throbbing with sincerity, 'but I want to be sure that Rhys has found the right woman for him. He's such a special person.'

'I know he is,' said Thea evenly. 'That's why I'm in love with him.'

'Ah, then you *do* understand that!'

As opposed to not understanding everything else? Thea wondered with rising irritation. Perhaps it was time to go on the offensive.

'Are you trying to say that you don't think I am the right woman for him?'

Lynda held up her hands. 'Please, Thea, don't get defensive. I'm only trying to ensure that you and Rhys don't make a terrible mistake. It may be that you are meant for each other but, if not, it's surely better to find out now. Nobody knows better than I do what agony divorce can be.'

Thea thought about her sister, who probably knew just as much about the pain of divorce as Lynda, who had waltzed off of her own accord.

'What exactly makes you think that we might be making a mistake?' she asked coldly.

'It's just one or two things Kate said that made me wonder,' said Lynda, still oozing warmth and sincerity.

Thea eyed her with acute dislike. 'Really?' she said. 'What kind of things?'

'We-ell, she mentioned that you were a secretary, for a start.'

'Yes, I work for a PR firm. Is that a problem?'

'Oh, not a *problem* as such. It's just that Rhys has always been a bit of an intellectual. I remember I used to feel quite intimidated by him sometimes.' She gave a little trill of laughter as if to show that she knew how incredible this seemed. 'He's got a marvellous mind,' she added earnestly. 'He's someone who really needs an intellectual equal.'

Right, so that ruled Thea out, obviously.

She wondered about telling Lynda about her degree, but decided not to bother. It wouldn't make any difference.

Lynda could talk all she liked about wanting Rhys to be happy, but to Thea it was pretty clear that she had no intention of letting him out of her sphere of influence. She didn't want to be married to him herself, but she didn't want anyone else to have him either. In Lynda's world, Rhys belonged firmly on the end of her string, to be jerked whenever she chose.

Just like Harry and Isabelle.

It turned out that she wasn't cosmopolitan enough for Rhys either. A few holidays on the Continent and a trip to New York didn't make her a suitable companion for a man as well-travelled as Rhys, it seemed.

'I feel he really needs someone who has spent some time in developing countries and is used to expatriate life,' said Lynda.

'He's not an expatriate now,' Thea couldn't help pointing out. 'He's living in Wimbledon!'

Lynda frowned a little at her obtuseness. 'I don't think that's quite the point, Thea.'

From upstairs, Thea could hear the scraping of Sophie's violin. She wished the two of them would come down and rescue her.

'What exactly *is* the point?'

'The point is that to be really happy Rhys needs someone with a similar background and experiences to his. You can't just start from scratch. I always think the history each person brings to a relationship is almost as important as the present. Don't you agree?'

Thea thought about Harry again. 'As a matter of fact, I do, yes.'

'I mean, holiday romances are all very well, but when it comes down to it, it's being able to share the important experiences of life that makes the strongest bond. Things like marriage and having children. You just can't understand what that's like until you've been there. You, for instance, have never been married, have you, Thea?'

'No.'

'And you haven't got any children?'

'No.' Thea felt as if she were failing spectacularly at an important interview. 'But I really like children,' she offered, hating herself for sounding as if she was seeking approval. 'I spend a lot of time with my niece.'

'Ye-es.' Lynda's lack of enthusiasm was perfectly judged. 'I've heard a lot about Clara. She's obviously given a lot more freedom than Sophie is used to.'

The subtext being that Thea was clearly irresponsible and an unfit person to be in charge of children. Thea bit back an angry retort.

'I'm just trying to say that you don't always have to have had a baby to know about children.'

'No, but it's not the same, is it? You can have no idea of what it's like to hold your newborn baby in your arms, or to see them take their first steps. Rhys does. That's something you can't share with him.

'It's not your fault,' Lynda went on so patronisingly that it was all Thea could do not to grind her teeth. 'The fact is that, as far as the important things in life are concerned, you and he don't share much common ground, and I'm not sure that bodes well for a long-term relationship, let alone marriage. Sharing the same kind of experiences, the same kind of life, the same way of thinking…these things are fundamental to any strong relationship.'

Thea took a defiant slurp of her wine, but her heart was sinking.

The very worst thing was that Lynda was right.

'I think you should ask yourself what you and Rhys really have in common,' said Lynda in that hateful gentle voice that made Thea want to stand up and scream.

This was Sophie's mother, though, so she couldn't do that. She looked at the sapphires gleaming on her finger instead and thought about Rhys, about those long sunny days and the starlit nights and the way his smile warmed her. She thought about how safe she felt when she was with him and the deep thrill that ran through her whenever he touched her and the terrible emptiness when he had gone.

Lifting her eyes, she looked directly at Lynda. 'We love each other,' she said.

Lynda sighed regretfully. 'Sometimes love isn't enough. I'll be honest with you, Thea,' she said. 'I was rather afraid that Rhys would do something like this.'

'Like what?'

'Get involved with someone on the rebound from our divorce.'

Thea gaped at her. 'You've been divorced five years! It's a bit late for a rebound, isn't it?'

'Not if you think that Rhys has been in something of a limbo since then. He's only been back in the country a few weeks. You must be about the first woman he has had the chance to meet.'

'Oh, I didn't realise there weren't any women in Morocco.'

'Sarcasm is a very negative reaction, Thea,' said Lynda reproachfully. 'Remember, I'm only trying to help. I care too much about Rhys to want him to get involved in something that might only hurt both of you.'

If she was waiting for Thea to thank her for her concern, she had a long wait ahead of her. Thea set her chin stubbornly.

'Rhys came back to get to know Sophie properly before it's too late,' Lynda went on, evidently abandoning hope of any gratitude on Thea's part. 'He's got a lot of years to make up for, and I think it's best if he does that before he gets involved with anyone else.'

It was all sounding very familiar. Had the whole concentrate-on-Sophie idea come from Lynda in the first place? It was a perfect way for her to maintain her influence without actually going to the bother of marrying Rhys again. The first sign that another woman might become part of his life, and all Lynda had to do was press the guilt button. Oh, yes, Thea could see it all.

She wasn't about to give Lynda the satisfaction of admitting that she was beaten, though. She smiled sweetly at the other woman.

'*I* think it's best that Rhys decides for himself,' she said. 'I can understand why you're concerned about Sophie, but all I can tell you is that I love her, and I love Rhys. I love him very much, and I want to spend the rest of my life with him. It might not—'

Thea broke off as Lynda's great dark eyes widened suddenly, and she looked over her shoulder to see Rhys standing in the doorway.

'How long have you been there?' asked Lynda sharply.

Rhys smiled. 'Long enough.' He came into the room to stand behind the sofa where Thea was sitting and rested his hand at the nape of her neck, and she closed her eyes in involuntary pleasure at the warmth of his touch. 'I love you, too,' he said softly.

CHAPTER TEN

THEA was quiet as they walked back towards the station. It had stopped raining by then but the sky was still dull and grey.

Like her spirits.

In spite of her fragile appearance, Lynda was a strong woman. It was clear that she wanted to keep Rhys close to home, and she wasn't about to let Thea interfere. Thea didn't think that she was jealous. For all her talk about caring, she hadn't got the impression that Lynda was still in love with Rhys, or wanted him back.

No, it just suited her to have him around. Thea could see how flattering it would be for Lynda to believe that he was inconsolable. To be able to imply, as she obviously had to Kate, that he had never really got over her.

The role of lost love was perfect for Lynda, and she wouldn't give it up easily. It wouldn't be quite so convincing if Rhys was demonstrably happy with somebody else though, was it? No wonder she was keen to suggest—with the best possible motives, of *course*—that he wasn't ready for any relationship.

The question was, did Thea love Rhys enough to take Lynda on?

It was easy to see what would happen. Lynda would be all sweetness and light, but whenever Thea had a special dinner planned there would be an urgent request for Rhys to have Sophie for the night. If they were going somewhere special, she would have forgotten to tell him about a PTA meeting, or a violin lesson that Lynda couldn't make, so could Rhys just drop everything and take Sophie instead?

And how could Thea complain if Rhys was being a good father? There was no way she could insist that he put her before his daughter. Of course he would have to go.

His guilt about Sophie gave Lynda a huge advantage, and Thea knew that she would play it for all it was worth. It wasn't even personal. Lynda would be the same with any woman who ventured into Rhys's life.

And Thea couldn't be sure that Rhys cared enough to do anything about it. She wasn't going to be silly and suspect that he was still in love with Lynda. That was just Lynda's propaganda. Rhys had said nothing to suggest that was the case.

On the other hand, he had said nothing to suggest that he was in love with her either. He was doing exactly what he said he wanted to do, and that was to make his daughter his priority.

That left Thea with a stark choice. She could stand up to Lynda and fight for Rhys. Or she could walk away and leave him until he worked out what he wanted himself.

She loved him. The truth of that rang deep inside Thea. It wasn't something she could analyse or explain, but in the very core of her being she felt that he was the only man she would ever love, the only man she would ever need. The thought of going through life without him was unendurable.

Thea had seen enough to know that a love like that was a very special thing, a gift, and not to be treated lightly. It was worth more than a 'maybe it will, maybe it won't work' approach. Shouldn't she do everything she could to give it a chance to flower and see if Rhys might come to feel the same?

But she was afraid. Afraid that too many last minute summonses from Lynda would sour any relationship that they managed to build. Thea could see herself growing snippy and resentful every time Rhys had to drop everything the moment Lynda decided to make him feel guilty about Sophie, and he would end up torn and exhausted by conflicting demands.

Just like Harry.

No, Thea had had enough of triangular relationships. They didn't work, she knew that to her own cost already.

Rhys would need to decide whether he wanted to make a new life for himself, and if he wanted her to be part of it, but she had to let him make that decision on his own. She had to stand aside now, or she would only get hurt, just like Lynda had said.

'You're very quiet,' said Rhys after a while.

'I'm sorry. I was just thinking.'

Thinking about how hopeful she had felt when she had dressed that morning. The thought of dinner with Rhys had held out so much promise, the chance of a new and wonderful life, loving and being loved the way she had always dreamed of being loved.

'You look sad,' he said. 'Were you thinking about Harry?'

Thea concentrated on fastening her umbrella. 'In a way, yes.'

'I thought you said you were OK about the way it had worked out?'

'I know, and I am really,' she said, picking her words with care. 'It's just that sometimes it's harder to put it all behind you than at others.'

Rhys hesitated. 'Do you want to talk about it?'

'I don't think I do now,' said Thea slowly, knowing that once she started to talk the truth would come out, and Rhys didn't need that. 'But thanks.'

'OK.' He nodded, accepting that immediately in a way

Harry would never have done. Harry would have pushed and pushed, and she would have found herself in tears and it would have ended with them both feeling guilty. 'Tell me how you got on with Lynda instead.'

'Ah, Lynda.' Thea put her head on one side, wondering how to put it. 'Let's just say that she's not sure our engagement is a good idea.'

'*What?*' To her surprise, Rhys sounded outraged. 'Lynda told me that she was thrilled for me!'

And he had obviously believed her. That was men for you.

'That was before she met me,' said Thea delicately. 'I gather she doesn't think I'm quite right for you.'

Rhys scowled. 'Why the hell not?' Anyone would think that he had forgotten all about the pretence, she thought with a pang.

'Well, we don't have that much in common when you come to think about it—as Lynda obviously has.' She glanced up at him. 'I thought you'd overheard that bit?'

'No,' he said. 'I only heard you say that you loved me.'

'Oh, that,' said Thea after a tiny pause. 'Did I sound convincing?'

'Very.'

Keep it light, she told herself fiercely. 'You didn't do so badly yourself. That hand on my neck was a master stroke, I thought.'

Rhys looked down at her, just as she risked another glance at him, and their eyes met for a brief moment before both looked away. For a while, there was silence, broken only by the sound of their footsteps on the pavement.

Rhys's mouth was set in an alarmingly grim line. 'What's it got to do with Lynda, anyway?' he demanded.

'It doesn't really matter, does it?' said Thea, determinedly avoiding meeting his gaze once more. 'In fact, I was thinking that it might be a good reason to end our engagement.'

'What would be?'

She had never heard Rhys sound so short before. Something had put him in a really bad mood, and she wasn't sure whether it made it easier for her or more difficult.

'The fact that we've got nothing in common.'

'Oh, that,' he said, echoing her words with a touch of sarcasm.

'You can say that we realised that she was right, and it would have been a mistake for us to marry.'

Lynda would like that, Thea thought wryly. It went against the grain to give her the satisfaction of thinking that they had taken her advice. On the other hand, they had successfully fooled her into believing that theirs was a genuine relationship, or she would never have gone to so much trouble to dissuade Thea from pursuing it. It was good to know that Lynda wasn't *that* perceptive, whatever Kate might claim for her famous insight.

They had reached the turning to the station. 'There's a nice little restaurant just down here,' said Rhys, nodding straight ahead. 'I was thinking we might go there.'

Thea took a deep breath. 'Actually, I think I'll pass on dinner if you don't mind.'

'Don't you want anything to eat?'

'I'm not really that hungry.' It was true, too, although Rhys might have trouble believing it after the way she had tucked into her food in Crete.

Rhys looked puzzled, as well he might. 'What about another night, then? How would Friday do for you?'

'I...don't think so,' said Thea with difficulty. 'Things are a bit complicated at the moment.'

'I see.'

An awkward silence fell. Biting her lip, Thea tugged the ring off her finger.

'I almost forgot. Here, you'd better have this back.'

Rhys made no move to take it from her. 'Why don't you keep it?' he said abruptly. 'Have it as a thank you.'

'What for?'

'For tonight. For Sophie.' He hesitated. 'For Crete.'

Thea swallowed. 'Rhys, I can't. It's much too expensive.' She tried a smile, but it wasn't a very successful one. 'I couldn't wear it anyway. It's an engagement ring.'

'No, you're right. Of course.' Rhys took the ring from her and put it in his jacket pocket.

'I'll...um...get the tube back from here, then,' she said after a painful moment.

'I'll see you home.'

'Don't be silly, it's still early. I'll be fine.'

Rhys insisted on walking her to the station, but she managed to dissuade him from taking her all the way home.

'Thank you for this evening,' he said formally as she attempted to fish out her travel pass.

Thea summoned another smile, not much more successful than the last one. 'It was nice to see Sophie again.'

Ah, there was her pass at last. She tried not to think about the last time she had been through the ticket barrier, and the way he had kissed her in front of everybody.

'Well... I'd better go,' she said.

'Goodbye, Thea.'

Rhys's face was set as he watched her put her ticket through the machine. On the other side, Thea hesitated, looking back at him, longing to push her way back through the barrier and tell him that she had changed her mind, that she would like to go out to dinner, and then for him to see her all the way home.

But every time it got more difficult to say goodbye. Better to make a clean break now than prolong the agony.

'Bye, then,' she said and lifted a hand before she made herself turn away and walk down to where a train was just pulling into the platform.

'But *why*?' asked Nell plaintively. 'You didn't even give him a chance to choose you over Lynda!'

'It's not a choice between me and Lynda. It's a choice between me and Sophie, and he has to choose Sophie.'

Thea sipped miserably at the tea Nell had made her when she had dissolved into tears on her doorstep.

'I'm sick of falling for men with all this emotional baggage,' she complained. 'Next time I fall in love, it's going to be with someone who doesn't have a past to screw him up!'

'You'd better start looking for a toy boy, then,' said Nell practically. 'Stick to men under twenty and you should be OK.'

'But I don't want a toy boy. I want a real man.'

Rhys, in fact.

Nell sighed. 'If you want a man of your own age, you're going to have to accept that he's going to come with an emotional history, Thea. Most normal men are going to have had at least one serious relationship by the time they hit their mid-thirties and, if they're available, the chances are that it's going to have ended in tears—just like yours did.

'Let's face it, we've all got emotional baggage. I certainly have, and you have too. If you hadn't been messed around by Harry, you wouldn't be scared of making a go of it with Rhys now.'

'I'm not scared,' Thea protested. 'I'm just trying to be realistic about the problems. I couldn't bear it if it all turned nasty and I turned into some horrible, bitter cow.'

'Well, then, you'll have to make sure that you don't let it turn nasty,' said Nell. 'Of course it would be difficult sometimes, but show me a relationship that isn't. If a relationship is worth having, it's worth working for.'

She paused, and then went on more gently, 'You know, not everyone is lucky enough to find someone they can love the way you love Rhys. You can't just walk away without even trying because you want some perfect story-book relationship. It's not like that, Thea. Sophie is always going to be part of Rhys. He wouldn't be the man he is without her, and she comes as part of the package. At least you like her and she likes you—that's a huge thing.'

'What about Lynda?' Thea had been so sure that walking away had been the sensible thing to do, and she had expected the ever-practical Nell to support her, not make her doubt that she had taken the right decision.

'She probably will be a bit difficult sometimes, but you can deal with that. You should feel sorry for her, not resent her.'

'*Sorry* for her? Why?'

'She's Rhys's past. You had a chance to be his future. I know which one I'd rather be.'

Thea knew what she wanted to be too, but she was terribly afraid that she had thrown away the one chance that she had, and as September slid into October and the leaves began to turn, she began to lose the little hope she had that Rhys would find that he missed her enough to try again.

She did her best to be cheerful, but it wasn't easy with this nagging ache inside her, this dullness lying on her heart, this dismal sense that however much effort she made the future stretched bleakly and interminably empty without him.

Nell worried about her. 'Why don't you ring him?'

'I can't. I've thought about it so many times. I even get

as far as picking up the phone sometimes, but what would I say? "I didn't really mean it when I said I was just pretending to be in love with you? Oh, and by the way, is that invitation to dinner still on?"'

'You could start by saying hello, and see where you went from there.'

'Nell, he's never said anything about loving me. Not once. We've never even kissed for real. It's always been part of some pretence. What if I'm just building up some relationship that doesn't really exist in my mind? If there *had* been something there, Rhys could have contacted me.'

'He probably thinks you aren't interested after you brushed him off about the restaurant,' Nell pointed out.

'I've decided to be fatalistic about it,' said Thea. 'If it's meant to be, it'll be. And if it's not, it'll probably be because Lynda's right. I mean, we *don't* have anything in common.'

Apart from a sense of humour. And memories of those starlit nights in Crete. And lips that seemed made for each other.

'No, Rhys needs to decide what he wants. If it's me, he'll get in touch. If it isn't... Well, I'll just have to get on with my life, won't I?'

She turned her head as the front door banged, glad of the excuse to change the subject. 'Is this Clara?'

'Yes, Simon said he'd bring her back. She's been bowling with Sophie, I think.'

Clara leapt on Thea when she saw her. 'I haven't seen you for ages and ages!'

'No, not for at least a week,' said Thea, hugging her before she added, super-casual, 'How's Sophie?'

'She's fine.'

Thea longed to ask about Rhys, but what would Clara know? She would just say that he was fine too, and Thea didn't want to know that. She wanted to know that he was thinking about her, that he was missing her, that his nights were as miserable and empty as hers.

Clara was helping herself to a biscuit from the tin on the table. 'Thea?' she said in a wheedling tone.

'Yes?' she said cautiously, wondering what was coming.

'Will you take me skating? There's a brilliant new ice rink and I need someone to help me. Dad won't do it, and Mum can't because of her ankle.'

'I haven't been skating for years, and even then I was useless,' said Thea. 'I could hardly stand upright. I don't think I'd be much help.'

'Oh, *please*,' begged Clara. 'It would be fun if you came.'

What else did she have to do? 'Oh, all right then. We'll go next weekend if you like.'

Clara was determined that she wouldn't forget her promise. She rang Thea twice during the week to make sure that she had remembered she was to pick her up on Saturday afternoon. 'Then we can get there about two-thirty, can't we?'

'I suppose so,' said Thea, puzzled. 'They won't close before then, surely?'

'No, but we want plenty of time,' said Clara vaguely.

'I'm a bit nervous,' Thea confessed to her sister when she turned up obediently on Saturday afternoon. 'I'm sure I'll never be able to stand up, and I don't want to break *my* ankle.'

There was an air of suppressed excitement about Nell, she realised belatedly, and looked at her sister more closely. 'What's up?'

'Nothing,' said Nell quickly. 'Ah, here's Clara. Are you ready?'

'As ready as I'll ever be,' said Thea, getting up. 'Wish me luck!'

To her surprise, Nell put her arms round her and hugged her tightly. 'Good luck, Thea.'

'Hey, I was just joking!'

Nell smiled mistily. 'Good luck, anyway.'

Thea forgot about her sister's odd behaviour when they got to the rink. She eyed the crowded ice dubiously as she put on her boots. 'I hope I can remember how to do this.' Glancing up, she saw that Clara was scanning the rink. 'Looking for someone?'

'No,' said Clara airily. 'Just...watching.'

They had rather a wobbly start, and Thea wasn't sure who was hanging on to who, but after a while she began to get the hang of it. It would have been easier if they didn't have to keep going round the other nervous skaters who were hugging the edge equally assiduously.

'Let's go over there, where there's more space,' said Clara suddenly, and before Thea could protest had towed her out into the centre.

'Clara, I don't think this is a good id—' Thea broke off as she saw the two figures heading straight towards them.

Rhys and Sophie.

Unprepared for the great lurch of her heart, Thea's legs gave way, and she fell smack on her bottom, taking Clara with her.

The two girls promptly dissolved into helpless giggles, which left Rhys to lean down a hand.

'I'm not sure I'm very steady myself,' he confessed, 'but I'll do my best.'

Clara had already scrambled up, and between them they got Thea upright, although her legs were trembling so much she didn't think they would stay that way for very long.

She couldn't take her eyes off Rhys. Paralysed by the fear that this would turn out to be a dream, she just stared and wondered what on earth she could say to keep him there. Then she remembered what Nell had said about simply saying hello and seeing where it took them.

'Hello,' she said shakily.

Rhys smiled at her. 'Hello.'

'Dad, Clara and I can skate together now,' said Sophie artlessly, 'so you and Thea can sit down if you want.'

'Thank God for that,' said Rhys, watching the two girls skate off, miraculously restored to competence. 'Well?' he said to Thea, who had hardly noticed they were gone. 'Do you think we can make it back to the side?'

'I might need to hang on to you,' she managed to say huskily, and Rhys took her firmly by the hand.

'If you hang on to me and I hang on to you, I think we'll make it,' he said.

Thea felt in a curious state of limbo as she took off her boots, still hardly able to believe what was happening. For a while she just sat there by his side, reliving that feeling of his hand closed firmly around hers, the blissful security of knowing that he was strong enough and steady enough to stop her falling.

It was almost as if the touch of his hand had said everything that needed to be said. As if everything had been explained and understood without saying a word. Thea could feel herself filling up with a warm and wonderful sense of certainty.

'Did Clara set this up?' she asked at last.

'I believe it was a joint effort. Sophie certainly chose the venue.' Rhys glanced around the echoing hall, at the crowded ice rink and the hard green plastic seats. 'I'm not sure she's quite got the hang of romance yet.'

'So you knew all about it?'

'Not until yesterday. I guessed something was up when I went to pick Sophie up from Clara's. I met your sister. She's nice, isn't she?'

'*Nell* knew?'

Thea remembered the brilliance of Nell's eyes earlier, the way she had hugged her and whispered, 'Good luck'. Of course she had known.

'She hadn't known long. The girls worked it all out themselves,' said Rhys. 'They were sure that we were both unhappy and they decided to do something about it.'

'*Have* you been unhappy?' asked Thea.

'Yes,' he said simply, looking into her eyes, his own very light and clear. 'I've missed you, Thea. I've missed you more than I would have thought possible.'

'I've missed you too,' she said and, when he held out his hand, she took it and held it tightly as the awful tightness around her heart began to ease.

'I'm in love with you,' said Rhys in the same direct way. 'I think I've been in love with you since you sat on our terrace that morning. You took that deep breath to smell the coffee, and you smiled at me, and I was lost.'

'Why didn't you say anything?'

'I didn't want to admit it, not even to myself. I didn't want to fall in love. I'd made up my mind that I was going to devote myself to Sophie, and I felt guilty about thinking about anyone except her, but it was so hard not to when you were there, smiling, talking, so easy to be with. I clung to the idea that it was all a pretence, and that it didn't really mean anything when I kissed you, but it got harder and harder to remember that it wasn't real.'

'I know,' said Thea with feeling, curling her fingers around his.

'Do you?' he asked seriously, and she nodded.

'Yes, I do, Rhys. I know exactly what it's like to fall in love with someone when you least expect to, when you don't really want to. When you think they're just pretending to be in love with you.'

'I didn't think you could love me.' Rhys sounded uncertain for the first time. 'I thought you were just pretending.'

A smile was tugging at the corners of Thea's mouth, and she ran her free hand up to his shoulder.

'I'm not pretending now.'

He kissed her then, a long sweet kiss on the hard plastic seats with the hissing ice and the shrieking children in the background, and Thea wound her arms around his neck and kissed him back as her heart swelled with happiness and joy spilt in a dizzying rush along her veins.

They were roused by the sound of clapping. Sophie and Clara were leaning on the edge of the rink, beaming with self-satisfaction. 'Can we be bridesmaids?'

Rhys sighed. 'Go away,' he said, without taking his arms from around Thea. 'I haven't asked her to marry me yet.'

'Oh, Dad, what have you been *doing*?' Sophie rolled her eyes. 'You will, won't you, Thea?'

Thea started to laugh. 'Who's making the proposal here?'

'Well, you did say you would prefer being proposed to in public rather than in a boring candlelit restaurant,' Rhys reminded her. He made to get up. 'Would you like me to find a microphone and everybody can watch?'

'No!' Half laughing, half horrified, Thea caught at his sleeve and pulled him back down beside her. 'No, it's quite public enough here with just the four of us!'

'All right then. Will you marry me, Thea?'

'Say yes,' hissed Clara.

'Yes,' said Thea obediently.

'And now will you go away?' Rhys said to the two girls. 'It would be nice to kiss Thea without an audience for once.'

'Ooh,' chorused the girls, but they waggled their hands and skated away, their mission accomplished.

'Don't forget the ring, Dad,' Sophie shouted over her shoulder.

'What ring?' mumbled Thea a few minutes later as she emerged from his kiss. 'You must have been very sure of me!'

'No,' said Rhys, suddenly serious. 'I was just very hopeful. Anyway, it's just this old thing.' He pulled out a familiar box and took the sapphire ring out to slip it back on to Thea's finger. 'I'm not sure whether Lynda would have noticed if you were wearing it or not that evening. That was just an excuse. I just wanted to see you wearing my ring. When you gave it back that night it felt like a slap in the face.'

'I'm sorry,' said Thea, kissing him to make up for it. 'I won't give it back again.'

They sat on, oblivious to the cold, while Sophie and Clara whizzed around the ice rink, well pleased with their afternoon's work. Thea snuggled into Rhys's side.

'We've wasted so much time!' she said with a sigh. 'Why didn't you tell me how you felt in Crete?'

'I thought you were still in love with Harry,' he pointed out. 'You'd been very honest about him, and it seemed as if you were just being nice about taking part in the pretence. I didn't feel as if I could tell you, and anyway, I wasn't even that sure how I *did* feel then. I kept telling myself that it was just a holiday romance and that I'd get over it when I got home, but I didn't. I couldn't get you out of my mind, so when Lynda asked to meet you I jumped at the excuse to see you again.

'When I did, I realised it wasn't just Crete,' he said, laying his palm against her cheek and turning her head so that he could look into her glowing grey eyes. 'It was you. It'll always be you.'

He kissed her softly, sealing the promise.

'You could have said something then,' said Thea when she had kissed him back.

'I was going to. I thought it would be best if I tried to start again, like a proper relationship, so I suggested dinner, and I thought it was all going to be OK, especially when I met you at the tube. But then you backed off after meeting Lynda.'

She had, Thea remembered guiltily. 'Is that why you seemed so angry?'

'I was angry. I was angry with her for interfering, angry with you for letting her put you off, and angriest with myself for getting in such a mess and handling it all so badly. You were still preoccupied with Harry, or at least that's what you made me think, so I decided I should just leave things for the time being and concentrate on Sophie.

'The trouble was that I couldn't concentrate properly when Sophie kept talking about you. She was always asking when we would see you again, if we could go on holiday again… She kept saying how much she liked you and how much fun it had been when we were engaged, until I couldn't bear it any longer. I told her that you were in love with someone else and hadn't got over it, so that was the end of it.'

'Poor Sophie.'

Rhys snorted. 'Poor Sophie wasn't about to accept that it was the end of it at all. She reported everything back to Clara, who had apparently decided that you and I were both being very silly and that if we'd had any sense we would have made the engagement a real one while we were still in Crete.'

'I hate the way Clara's always right,' said Thea, resting her face against his shoulder.

'Anyway, Clara told Sophie that you weren't in love with Harry any more at all.'

'*I* told you that too!'

'You didn't tell me that Harry had wanted to get back

together with you and that you'd said no. I was under the impression that you were still nursing a broken heart, but when Sophie told me that I began to wonder why you hadn't taken him back when you had the chance. And then it wasn't a very big step to hoping that you'd discovered that you didn't really love him at all.'

'I didn't,' said Thea, nuzzling his throat. 'I was far too much in love with you by then.'

She felt Rhys smile into her hair and then bend his head to kiss her again, another long, long kiss that left her breathless and dizzy with happiness.

'Are you sure?' he asked. 'I don't want you to feel that you were bullied into marrying me by those girls.'

Thea thought about the reasons she had decided to walk away at the tube station that day, and then she thought about what Nell had said, about not letting true love slip through her fingers because she wasn't prepared for some hard times. Nell had told her that she had to make a choice, and Thea was making it now. She wanted to be Rhys's future, not his past.

'Yes, I'm sure,' she said. 'Are you?'

'Absolutely.'

'What about Sophie?' she persevered a little hesitantly. 'I don't want you to feel torn between us.'

'You saw how keen Sophie was for us to get married,' said Rhys. 'I don't think she's going to feel left out, and she won't be. I thought I would feel guilty about that, but I had a long talk with your sister when I picked Sophie up yesterday, and she said a very wise thing.'

'What was that?'

'She said that the best thing I could do for Sophie was to give her the example of a loving relationship. She said Sophie needed to see that adults could live together and laugh together and love together. How else would she learn to do that herself when she was grown up?'

Good old Nell.

'You said once that we didn't have anything in common,' Rhys went on. 'It's true that you don't know much about rocks and I don't know much about shoes, but I can't imagine living and laughing and loving with anyone but you, Thea. If we've got that in common, we don't need anything else, do we?'

'No,' said Thea, pulling his head down for another kiss, 'we don't.'

Thea stood in the panelled room and watched the children running around, thoroughly over-excited after the wedding ceremony and wilder still at the prospect of hanging up their stockings when they got home.

The hotel had been beautifully decorated for Christmas. A great fire burned at one end of the room, the leaping flames casting jumping shadows over the gleam of gold on her finger, while a spectacular Christmas tree stood at the other, spangled with lights and hung with gold and silver baubles.

She stepped back as a gaggle of flushed and giggling children ran past, Sophie and Clara in the thick of it all as usual. Both girls were wearing bridesmaids' dresses in a deep, warm green colour that suited their vivid personalities much better than a pastel shade would have done.

Thea had imagined them each wearing a simple Christmas rose in their hair, but their hearts had been set on the little tiaras they had spotted in the wedding shop, and in the end she had given in. It was hard to resist when she was constantly being reminded that if hadn't been for them she wouldn't be getting married at all.

She herself was wearing a suit of ivory shot silk, but the

unaccustomed elegance ended there. Defying even the hairdresser's ministrations, her hair rioted about her face as normal, but she had decided to opt for the natural look. On a day like this, even her hair didn't matter.

Oops! Thea nearly spilt her glass of champagne as Damian—or was it Hugo?—cannoned into her, in hot pursuit of the others.

'We've got to invite Kate,' she had said to Rhys. 'If it hadn't been for her, we might never have thought of a Christmas wedding.'

They might never have pretended to fall in love.

They might never have done it for real.

And she might not be standing here now, with a brand new ring on her finger, and a brand new husband talking to her father a few feet away.

Thea could see Kate and Nick talking to Nell now. Kate had been gracious, if a little disapproving at the speed with which the wedding had been arranged.

'Two months!' she had exclaimed. 'I wonder you found anywhere—and on Christmas Eve too!'

'We were lucky the hotel had a cancellation.'

'Very lucky,' Kate had said, so obviously torn between satisfaction at getting another couple of singletons married off and a certain irritation that they had managed to arrange everything perfectly without her advice, that Thea had had to suppress a smile.

'What are you smiling about?' Rhys slipped an arm around his bride and she kissed him.

'I was just thinking about luck,' she said.

'That's funny, *I* was just thinking what luck it was that you're standing right where you are.'

'Standing…?' Puzzled, Thea followed his glance upwards to where a huge bunch of mistletoe hung from the chandelier. Several guests had stopped and were watching, smiling as they realised his intent too, and she laughed.

'Don't you think that just once, Rhys, you could kiss me in private, without an audience?' she said with mock severity.

Rhys smiled as he drew her into his arms. 'Later,' he promised.